Forever and Beyond

Ancient Legends

JAYDE SCOTT

Other titles in the Ancient Legends series

A Job From Hell
Beelzebub Girl
Voodoo Kiss
Dead And Beyond
Shadow Blood

Other titles by Jayde Scott

Black Wood
Mortal Star
The Divorce Club
Born to Spy

©Copyright 2012 Jayde Scott
The right of Jayde Scott to be identified as the author of this work has been asserted in accordance with the Copyright, Designs and Patents Act 1988.

All rights reserved. No part of this publication may be reproduced, stored in a retrieval system, or transmitted in any form or by any means, electronic, mechanical, photocopying, recording or otherwise, without the prior permission of the author.

This is a work of fiction and any resemblance between the characters and persons living or dead is purely coincidental.

All rights reserved.
ISBN: 1479130664
ISBN-13: 978-1479130665

For Foxy, Silver and Tabby

You taught me the true meaning of love …

Acknowledgments

First and foremost my gratitude goes out to my spouse for the immense support, endless love and for being my soul mate even during a writer's dark and not so proud moments. I appreciate each and every second we get to spend together and hope our love will last for eternity.

Thank you to my kitties, who gift me with tons of laughter each and every day.

A huge thank you to my editor, Shannon, for all her input and long hours. Thank you also to my critique partners and fellow authors, and in particular Christine Peebles.

And, last but not least, a huge thanks to all my wonderful readers. This book wouldn't exist without your encouragement and Facebook messages.

Prologue

The Swiss Alps - 5 a.m.

In the snowy mountains of Switzerland there is a tiny village called Winterheim. Not many tourists find their way here because thick blankets of snow and blizzard-like winds make an ascent almost impossible, which suits the villagers just fine. They are private people, even hostile to visitors, if you will—protective of a secret Winterheim has been hiding for years: a tiny bakery named Magic Cupcakes.

Legend says the bakery is the home of the most powerful Seer that shall ever be born, the one that will decide over the fate of the world. The coming bloodshed will claim many lives. It will be a war of destruction and reorder, of domination and submission, and hunting humans will become a sport if the wrong court wins. And so the Seer must be protected at all costs. But how do you protect someone who was never meant to be born?

**

Even though dawn had yet to shoo away the impenetrable darkness of the mountains, inside Magic Cupcakes, eighteen-year-old Patricia had been awake for at least an hour, doing what she always did day in, day out: bake another tray of delicious hot buns, muffins, and cookies. She pushed a stray strand of her red, curly hair out of her tired eyes and sprinkled powder sugar on top of the strawberry tarts that always sold out within a few minutes after opening shop for the day, then hurried to get the cinnamon bread out of the oven before it turned dry.

Something prickled the nape of her neck. Irritated, she stepped aside, thinking it was her cat, Prince Rasputin. He was always up to no good when it came to snatching a bit of food, but Patricia had no time for the Hell demon's shenanigans. The tingling sensation returned, followed by something hot pressing against her skin and sending shivers of pleasure down her spine. Now, *that* she couldn't attribute to a mischievous cat. She smiled and turned to meet Kieran's experienced lips. He wrapped his arms around her chubby waist and pulled her into his strong arms, their mouths connecting in a long and deep kiss. Eventually, she pulled away, breathless, and trailed her fingers through his shaggy, dark hair as she heaved a long sigh.

"You gotta go already?"

He nodded, gravely. The golden glow of the flames burning inside the stoves caught in his impossibly blue gaze. "I do, pumpkin. But I'll be back as soon as I can."

"When are you going to tell them?" She snuggled against his broad chest, her soft body melting into his, and inhaled deeply, as though to etch his scent forever in her mind.

"As soon as everything's sorted out in Morganefaire," Kieran said. "Until then you stay here, safe."

"Be careful," she said, marveling at how strong he seemed and how much she loved being near him.

"I will." As he turned away from her, ready to leave her world, a sense of urgency grabbed hold of her heart. As a Seer, she could foretell the future, just not her own and that of her soul mate. That bothered her more than the curse dangling like a Damocles sword over her head.

***

City of Morganefaire - 3 a.m.

The church bell rang three times, signaling a full hour. Maya Mallory drew a long breath as she hurried her pace past the closed windowpanes to the high gates stretching against the canvass of the night. The travellers would be arriving soon and she wanted to be ready to greet them, show them to their quarters, and fetch them whatever they needed. Where she came from, being late wasn't an option.

The cold night air whipped her dark, straight hair against her skin; her charcoal gray dress clung to her thin body as she pushed her way forward against the biting wind. Eventually, she reached the south gate—an imposing structure made of stone and enforced by magic—and peered through the tiny opening into the darkness extending beyond the city. The unpaved street with tall trees to both sides seemed deserted, the dust settled. Then again, the group of vampires surely wouldn't arrive by foot. According to various ancient legends, they could shift from one location to another in the blink of an eye. At twenty-two summers old, Maya was too young to have seen it with her own eyes or even meet a vampire in person, but she believed the stories. In fact, she had been looking forward to this moment ever since she entered the Academy of Witchcraft. The fact that her hard work had paid off and she was entrusted with the honor to finally meet a creature of the night filled her with both anticipation and terror. Were they as beautiful yet terrible as legend said? She sure hoped so.

With a soft groan, she grabbed hold of the heavy iron bolt latch and opened the gate half a foot to peer into the night. The flickering torch barely reached the impenetrable darkness stretching over the nearby bushes and past the tall trees and high mountains surrounding Morganefaire. Maya swallowed hard to stifle the sudden sense of uneasiness settling in the pit of her stomach. It wasn't like a witch to fear the darkness, and yet she couldn't help herself. Her hand wandered to the dagger bound to her waist, her strong fingers clasping the hard leather tight as she peered up to the moon hidden behind thick clouds. Only a few hours until dawn. They had to be here any minute because everyone knew vampires couldn't travel in broad daylight...unless the rumors were true and the clan leader, Aidan McAllister, the first vampire ever to walk the surface of the earth with no fear of the sun and no need for blood would be honoring them with his visit.

A chilly wind ruffled the nearby bushes, jerking Maya out of her thoughts. She rubbed her palms together to keep her fingers warm, and focused on her surroundings again. Nothing stirred. No sign of any approaching visitor. Aidan was known for his punctuality. Her nerves unsettled her. She took a hesitant step forward and scanned the area for the umpteenth time.

Still nothing stirred.

She heaved a big sigh and stepped back when movement to her right caught her attention. Startled, she unconsciously pressed a hand against her racing heart and called out as her gaze tried to see beyond the dark veil of the night. "Hello?" She listened for any sign of life. The night remained as silent as a tomb.

Eerily silent.

It wasn't natural. Usually, you could at least hear the buzzing sound of fireflies or the wind's howling through the trees.

Maya held her breath until her lungs hurt from the lack of oxygen. A minute passed. Then another. When nothing happened, Maya breathed out, realizing her jumpiness was unfounded. She knew there was nothing to worry about. Morganefaire was safer than any other place in the world...or as safe as it could be for a witch.

A sudden movement in the bushes startled Maya. She turned her head sharply as something hard swung at her, hitting her hard in the back, knocking the oxygen out of her lungs. Gasping for air, she tumbled forward as she turned to look at her attacker. In the few seconds she had left, she realized it was a tall figure with a long cape and a black hood covering most of his face. Someone shorter and of a more delicate frame—probably female—stood a step behind him, next to a third hooded person.

She had been told to look out for three visitors: two male, one female. For a moment Maya's brain harboured the thought that maybe the guests didn't recognize her as a witch and mistook her for an intruder. Or why else would they attack her? She opened her mouth to explain when the hooded man lifted his hand and she looked into the dark reflection of a mirror. She felt the pull instantly and her soul began to shift within the confinement of her mortal body. Her first impulse was to scream, to run away and warn the others. She had heard the stories of a mirror that was once shattered into four fragments, each able to entrap a powerful soul. No one knew who the four powerful souls were but, as a witch, Maya always thought they'd be immortals—vampires, fallen angels, demons, maybe even Shadows, or deities with abilities reaching far beyond her imagination. She certainly never figured someone might ever try to entrap her soul.

Her brain commanded her legs to move but she didn't budge from the spot. A long scream remained trapped in her throat. She clung to her consciousness as she frantically tried to push the mirror away from her, but somehow she couldn't grab hold of it and her fingers kept slicing through the air.

Her powers began to wane, her will weakened. Fear surged through her veins. Mesmerized, as if under hypnosis, she inched closer to the hooded figure. Her fingers finally touched the cold surface of the mirror as her gaze remained glued to it. One of the three attackers whispered something and a freezing sensation crept under her skin and into her bones. For a moment, it hurt so badly she thought she'd die on the spot, but then the pain subsided and gave way to a new sensation: a sweet, delicious tiredness that drew her in and made her want to close her eyes and let it envelop her until she could no longer feel the world around her.

At the periphery of her mind she was aware of a girl's presence. Maya turned her head to the side and caught a glimpse of eyes as blue as the ocean and hair as black as the night. The girl was dangling from silver ropes, her skin covered in a sheet of frost that branched in all directions. Her lips shimmered bluish, making it impossible to tell whether she was just a beautiful marble statue, or alive and forever captured in the shard of the mirror.

And then another jolt sent Maya stumbling forward and the girl disappeared.

"We got the wrong witch," a deep male voice said.

"It doesn't matter," another male voice said, this one younger. "We'll keep looking until we find the right. What are we to do with this one?"

"Kill her," a woman said. "She looks like she'll talk."

"That's a bad idea, unless you want the whole city on guard," the younger male voice said.

A pause before the first male voice answered, "Let her live. I might just have the fitting mission for her. While we continue our search, she'll help us get back what is ours."

Maya shook her head vehemently and began to tug at the invisible chains holding her prisoner in her own body. The Council had instructed her to greet the visitors and attend to them in the guest quarters until further notice. Maya was determined to do as she was told, and nothing else. She didn't want to be part of anyone's mission.

"Stop struggling, or I might just have to hurt you," the female voice hissed in her ear.

She felt the woman's cold touch, how her fingers seemed to send electric impulses through her body, making her shake uncontrollably. At first, Maya thought she was on the verge of blackening out from fear, until she noticed that with each jolt, she was pushed nearer and nearer to a bottomless pit and the darkness around her deepened. But it wasn't the darkness that scared her. It was the feeling of being shoved and kicked when she couldn't move from the spot.

And then she understood what was happening. The woman was forcing her way inside Maya's body. Slowly, she could feel the woman's presence all around her—her thoughts, her feelings—pushing Maya's soul aside to make room for herself. A moment later, Maya lost all control over her body.

Somewhere in the distance footsteps approached and someone rattled at the gates. *Too late.* She could feel a smile tugging at her lips, even though she didn't want to smile. Her legs began to move slowly, clumsily, as though she was a child learning to take her first steps. But it wasn't Maya walking towards the visitors. It was *the other one* living inside Maya's body that greeted them at the gates.

Maya opened her mouth to scream for help but the sound remained trapped in her throat, and she knew she had lost the battle.

Chapter 1

The very first vacation with your boyfriend is a trial for any new relationship. Whether you want it or not, it's bound to cause you a few wrinkles. In my case, I was quite lucky because, as a newly turned vampire, I wouldn't have to worry about the appearance of my skin for the next five hundred years or so. Unfortunately, my new immortal status didn't protect me from my boyfriend's sarcasm and my consequent stubbornness caused by his unwillingness to understand a woman's needs.

Prior to our departure, Aidan had been pacing up and down our bedroom, shooting me annoyed glances from the corner of his stunning sapphire blue eyes. I knew he wanted me to hurry up and finish packing, but I wouldn't let a man haste me. So the more annoyed he became, the less inclined I felt to hurry up.

Eventually, he heaved a sigh and slumped down on the bed, propping his hands behind his head as he mumbled, "I don't know how many times I have to tell you it's not a vacation, Amber. We're going to Morganefaire on a job duty, basically to save our race. So, please, babe, for the sake of humanity, hurry up." His words were slow and emphasized, thick with a Scottish accent I had grown to love. His voice was low and imploring, but there was an edge to it I wouldn't mistake in a million years: Aidan was nervous. Coming from the guy who never lost his cool, I knew there was a lot at stake. Times were changing. The races were preparing for war and would stop at nothing in their quest to win the upper hand. Aidan was right to worry, and yet I couldn't help myself. I just couldn't decide what to pack. Light for sunny weather or thick for the Scottish Highlands and their unpredictable winds and sudden rainfalls?

"Where in England is Morganefaire located?" I asked, unfazed.

Aidan rubbed his forehead, avoiding my gaze. "Somewhere in the south. No one knows the exact location."

Yet more rain then, interspersed with the odd sunny day. With autumn approaching fast, the nights would cool down noticeably. While my body couldn't freeze to death, I just didn't like that tingly sensation in my limbs, so I rummaged through my cupboard and tossed a few thick sweaters and knitwear into my overstuffed suitcase, then jumped on top of it to close it while trying to shovel inside everything that spilled over the edges.

"You know we're not moving there, right? It's only for a couple of days. If you need anything we can just buy it or teleport back to get it."

I nodded, ignoring him, because the guy didn't get it. You don't pack what you need; you pack what you *think* you will probably need, taking into account each and every possibility, and then add some more stuff...just in case.

"Need help?" Aidan asked, smirking.

"Nah. I'm good," I grunted, wishing my pride wouldn't stop me from admitting I needed help indeed. Five minutes and a few more grunts later, I finally managed to zip up the darn thing and looked up at Aidan. "I think I'm ready."

A tiny flicker of hope sparkled in his eyes. "Really? I mean, are you sure? We're only a few hours late."

I smacked his bulging biceps and pointed at the suitcase. He heaved it up with a fake groan and dropped it onto the floor with a thud that reverberated from the mansion's old walls. For a moment, I thought I might be exaggerating a bit, but any doubts evaporated into thin air as soon as Aidan's brother, Kieran, teleported right in front of us, carrying a suitcase at least double the size of mine.

"You think you have enough, Kieran?" I said. "Geez, we're only going to be gone a few days."

Aidan met my gaze. "Yeah, some people just don't get it."

"You think?" I playfully slugged his arm, catching on to his subtle sarcasm.

"Think?" Aidan asked, smirking. "I *know*."

Kieran shrugged, his blue eyes sparkling. "I packed lightly. Only bare necessities." I had no doubt he believed every word he said.

"You've got to be kidding me," Aidan mumbled. "What's in there? A dead body?"

Kieran grinned and winked at me. "Nope, that one's in the other suitcase waiting in the hall."

Aidan shook his head grimly and walked past. I couldn't help but join in Kieran's laughter, thankful to have him around to ease up the tension. Visiting the witches' town was a huge deal for all of us, so any morsel of humor was highly welcome. I was positive Kieran would provide lots of that.

Chapter 2

When we finally left the safety of Aidan's mansion in the Scottish Highlands and gathered in the driveway, ready to teleport to the one place that could change the course of history, it was almost dawn. Up until recently, I had never heard of Morganefaire or the witches living there, so I was excited at the prospect of meeting others that belonged to the supernatural world. Granted, I was still pretty much clueless since no one bothered to brief me, as usual, but I couldn't quite shake off the feeling that I wouldn't find a pretty, medieval town with friendly, old ladies selling bogus love potions in tiny shops.

One of my best friends, Clare, wrapped her arms around me and pulled me in a tight hug. "Take care of the guys," she whispered in my ear, her long, blonde hair stroking my skin like silk.

"I will," I said, choking on an unshed tear. Clare was the only one of us who still suffered from bloodlust and had to fear the sun, meaning she had to stay behind and protect Aidan's property. With an encouraging smile I slowly pried myself from Clare to regard her pale face with delicate features and sparkling eyes that looked like she couldn't hurt a fly, but looks can be deceiving. Clare was the predator I'd never be, but she wasn't invincible. Ever since one of my friends—Angel—disappeared a few days ago, I had been on edge. If my brief time in the paranormal world had taught me anything it was that an immortal's life resembled Russian Roulette: one twist of fate and your old life was over in seconds. I could only hope Clare and I would meet again.

"Good luck." Clare waved before disappearing inside the house.

"Ready?" Aidan asked, grabbing my hand. I nodded and closed my eyes in the hope it might help ease the oncoming turmoil in the pit of my stomach. The air charged around us, then turned like a spiral, faster and faster, making my whole body protest until I thought I might just bend over, ready to puke, or faint on the spot, whichever came first. And then the sensation cleared and I dared to take a deep breath as I opened my eyes to take in my surroundings.

Even though the only source of light came from the huge waxing moon hanging low in the sky, my gaze adjusted quickly, giving me a sharper view than that of any mortal's. A long, unpaved street had replaced Aidan's driveway. We were surrounded by trees and bushes that cast ominous shadows in the night, beyond which I could make out the contours of high mountains interspersed with valleys. A tall wall blocked the view of what lay behind it, but I could sense it was the city. The knowledge unnerved me. Especially when my supernatural ears picked up faint, spooky, echoing breaths.

Aidan motioned us to follow as he led us to a closed gate. "This is the entrance."

"I'm ready to jump if you are," Kieran said.

Aidan shook his head. "You couldn't even if you wanted to."

"Speak for yourself," Kieran muttered but didn't press the issue.

I let my gaze trail around us as the nausea in the pit of my stomach subsided a little. The moon looked bigger here than in Scotland, with a bluish hue to it. I had never seen a Blue Moon in my life, but I remembered Aidan's words. It was a yearly occurrence that could only be seen in certain parts of the world, one that invited magic to be spun and pacts to be broken. This Blue Moon would be a special one, however, and time was running out. A powerful Seer foresaw that in just over a week it would start the war between the three races governing the paranormal world: the Shadows, the vampires, and the Lore Court ruled by the succubus demi-goddess Layla. Unfortunately, the Seer never revealed the outcome of the war. Or maybe the truth was so terrible it was best left unspoken.

After finding the Book of the Dead, which granted them full power over their spells and rituals, the Shadows—an immortal race of warriors and the vampires' archenemies—had been believed to be the most likely candidates to win. That is, until the vampires discovered their one weakness: the Shadows were nothing without their queen. After a vicious vampire attack, Deidre was now trapped in the body of a teen girl, growing weaker. A suitable vessel was chosen: a half-Shadow girl called Angel. Once she occupied Angel's body at the coming Blue Moon, Deidre would regain her full powers and lead her warriors to victory. Or so it was planned, until someone kidnapped Angel, knowing that without a vessel, Deidre would die eventually.

With the Shadows currently out of the picture, two courts were left to battle it out: the vampires and the Lore Court. Layla, a demi-goddess and the current ruler of the Lore Court, had begun to train more succubi, whose touch could be more fatal than a thousand swords. But she had her own problems to face: Layla's succubus mother had borne several children. Layla had done her best to hunt down and kill her half-siblings to ensure she kept her reign, but one escaped. Seth—half deity, half Shadow, and probably the biggest sociopath I had ever met—had been snubbed by the Shadows and was now ready to get rid of his sister and the Shadow queen to claim both the Lore and the Shadow throne for himself. But without an army, he had to rely on our cooperation. As much as I didn't trust the guy, we were too few in number to decline his 'help'. Besides, Layla still wanted my head after I won the Gift of Sight in her paranormal race. Aidan always thought if the chance presented itself, she'd kill us all. I had no doubt he was right.

Everyone was suiting up for war—everyone but us, which brings me to my kind: the vampires.

Ever since the Lore Court imprisoned the bloodthirsty and cruel vampire ruler, Flavius, the vampires were divided into factions that fought each other with a vengeance, meaning we were the weakest race out of the bunch. But Flavius's chances were increasing by the day. Aidan's maker, Rebecca, had found a way that might just help her free Flavius from his imprisonment. Legend told the story of an ancient mirror that was once broken into four shards. The one who combined the four fragments could open any portal and release whoever was trapped inside.

Yes, the paranormal world was changing, which was why we sought out Aidan's brethren in Morganefaire. We needed Morganefaire's magic if we wanted to stand a chance. I doubted the prophecy could be halted forever, but at least we could find out more about the ancient legends surrounding it and try to prevent Flavius's return.

"Are you still here?" Aidan whispered in my ear, jolting me out of my thoughts.

I nodded and smiled. "Yeah, I was just thinking about everything."

"That certainly explains the worry lines on your pretty forehead." He leaned in to place a soft kiss between my eyebrows, his breath lingering on my skin a tad too long. "Everything will be okay." His tone was strong, determined, but the edge in it didn't escape me.

The air smelled crisp and clean. A strong wind crept beneath my jeans and shirt, making me shiver, but not from the cold. It took me all of two seconds to realize what was wrong with this setting. It wasn't just the moon that was weird.

It was eerily quiet. No crickets sang in the grass, no owls hooted, and there was no noise from the city behind the walls.

"I think everyone's asleep," I said, rubbing my hands together nervously.

Aidan just frowned in response. I didn't like that. Usually, he at least *tried* to comfort me and make any strange occurrence seem like it wasn't a big deal.

"Either that, or they're dead," Kieran said. I let out a tiny gasp. Aidan elbowed him in the ribs. "What?" Kieran's eyebrows shot up. "She knows I'm kidding."

I tried to play it off. "Yeah, I knew."

"Balloons. Confetti. Champagne glasses," Kieran said sarcastically. "I guess they're pulling out all the stops to come out and greet their guests of honor."

Aidan shot him a warning look, silencing him instantly. "Follow me." With one arm he lifted my suitcase like it weighed nothing while the other moved around my waist to draw me close to him. It wasn't a gesture of affection. Aidan always did that when he thought he might need to protect me but didn't want to make it too obvious. I slapped his hand away playfully and stomped off in front of him. Kieran was right. Aidan was supposed to be some sort of guest of honor, and you don't greet your guests by snoring in your fluffy sheets.

Kieran hammered against the gate. I cringed at the noise, almost expecting half the city to wake up and start throwing buckets of water over our heads. But nothing moved.

"Hello?" I called out while pushing the gate hard. It didn't budge, even though it didn't even look as massive as I thought. "What the heck?"

"Magic," Aidan replied. "We have to wait like everyone else."

"I've never been a fan of sitting around and waiting for the Boogieman to come and get us," Kieran said, his nervous gaze darting to the left and right. His paranoia made me roll my eyes.

"What are you, like, five? There is no Boogieman."

He pointed at the almost full moon. "I'm talking about werewolves."

I shuddered but tried to play it off, as though it didn't bother me one tiny bit, not even after having a very close and intimate encounter with one of those. Claiming to be a Shadow, Brendan asked for my help when his girlfriend, Angel, disappeared and no one could find her. Eventually, the guy tried to eat me and almost succeeded. Up until the moment he attacked me I had no idea werewolves even existed, which made me wonder what else was out there.

When nothing stirred, I sat down under an oak tree and crossed my legs, prepared for a long wait. My hand reached out to touch the leaves dancing in the cool breeze. A change in subject was in order before the thought of werewolves and what else not gave me a few sleepless nights. "You were gone a while," I said to Kieran. "What happened with your baker girlfriend?"

"A gentleman doesn't talk." He slumped down next to me. The tiniest hint of a smile tugged at his lips and I knew he didn't even need encouragement to start talking about Patricia. "You want all the juicy details, don't you?" he asked.

"Yep!" I nodded as my gaze followed Aidan who was checking out the gate. He passed me a fleeting glance, followed by the cute frown he always sported when concentrating. He was thinking of ways to reach his brethren on the other side of the wall.

"So you can spill everything to your BFF Cass?" Kieran snorted. I turned to regard him. The soft skin around his eyes crinkled with laughter. His cheeks almost glowed—not in a sparkly way but with a radiant shimmer that could only mean one thing: he was in love. "No way," he said. "The next thing I know I'm hanging by my toe nails in one of her dad's dungeons in the deepest level of Hell." I laughed as I painted the picture before my eyes. Cass was Lucifer's daughter. Patricia was Lucifer's sister and thus Cass's aunt. She was also a Seer and bound to a haunted bakery, meaning her curse prevented her from ever leaving the place. Basically, if she so much as set one foot outside the door everyone around her would feel the sudden urge to kill her...until she married *the one*. As far as I knew, Kieran was her bonded mate, but he was also the worst player I had ever met. Then there was also the problem of Cass happening to hate Kieran with a vengeance. This was one affair that couldn't possibly last.

"My lips are sealed, I promise," I said. "So, did she tame the wild beast?"

He laughed. Aidan raised his brows, suddenly interested. Before Kieran could answer, I heard footsteps approaching.

"Saved by the bell," Kieran said.

Scrambling up, I peered into the darkness, but could make out nothing. A bolt slid and the gate opened slowly with a loud creak, just a tiny bit but enough to let me glimpse the face of a young woman, pale as a ghost with eyes as dark as rivers that seemed to swallow up the light. Her eyes shifted to and fro, focusing on nothing in particular.

"I'm Aidan McAllister. This is my girlfriend, Amber Reed, and my brother, Kieran McAllister." Though he spoke quietly, Aidan's smooth, dark voice oozed charm and confidence.

The woman's nervous gaze swept past Aidan and settled on me, examining me as though she'd never seen another female before. Her stare seemed unnatural, wooden, like that of a dead doll creeping you out because it looked like it might just get up and start talking any minute. I shivered again and averted my gaze, but I could feel her watching me closely for long seconds as the silence deepened around us.

"Maybe you don't know who we are," Aidan said eventually. His tone softened, trying to instill a sense of trust the way you do when talking with a fearful child. "In which case, get Blake." He spoke the name sharply, leaving no doubt that he had yet to forgive his former best friend's betrayal.

The woman's gaze eventually shifted away from me and focused on Aidan, ignoring Kieran completely. "I'm sorry, I wasn't aware it was you. Please come in." She spoke quietly, but something in her tone caught my attention. Her voice had a layer of fear to it, as though she was scared of us. I didn't have time to contemplate my thoughts because she pushed the gate open and stepped to the side to let us in.

I walked in after Aidan, followed by Kieran. The woman closed the gate quickly, then turned to face us. "My name's Maya. I'm responsible for your wellbeing and shall show you to your quarters. If you need anything during the length of your visit, I'm the one to contact."

The night bathed her face in complete darkness but my heightened vision picked up the unnatural glint in her eyes. I squinted to get a better look but she turned her back on me and took off down the cobblestone path through narrow streets, past dark buildings with closed shutters. She moved so swiftly I barely had enough time to shoot Aidan a questioning look. If he caught it, he didn't respond.

Chapter 3

The silence felt awkward, making me feel more like an intruder than a guest. We walked briskly for a few minutes, then stopped in front of an inconspicuous building that blended in with the others around it. As soon as we entered the hall, a jolt of electricity rushed through me. For a second, I thought I heard whispers coming from the hall behind us and I knew at once there was nothing normal about this place.

"Do you hear that?" I whispered.

Kieran arched a brow in enquiry. "Hear what?"

Aidan wrapped an arm around me and whispered, "Spirits might be trying to communicate with you. Just tune them out like we practiced."

I nodded and focused on telling them to come back another time. Soon the voices disappeared and I let out a sigh of relief.

"You speak to the dead?" Maya said. Her tone was sharp; her gaze was cold. There was something else. Hostility. Detest. I came to the conclusion she didn't like me very much. Maybe she believed all the rumors about vampires, that we were cruel, blood thirsty, callous barbarians. I couldn't blame her. More than half of us certainly fit the description, but I harbored no intention to become one of them.

"Unfortunately, yes." I curled my lips into a friendly smile in the hope she got the hint that I wanted to be her friend.

"Interesting." She turned her head to Aidan, ignoring me and Kieran. "These are the guest quarters. I hope everything's to your liking. If you need anything, you'll find me next door." She pointed to her right. I followed her line of vision and noticed the door obscured by a thin curtain—probably separate quarters reserved for members of staff. For some reason the way she talked to Aidan, emphasizing the word 'you' bothered me a little. Or maybe it was the way she regarded him too intently. Even though Aidan was my bonded mate, I couldn't help the pang of jealousy creeping up on me. I guess being a vampire didn't protect me from having the usual human feelings and insecurities.

"Thank you," Aidan said, oblivious to her behavior. "We can handle everything from here."

"I'll be back at eight a.m. unless—" She hesitated.

"That's perfect," Aidan said.

Maya nodded and disappeared into the darkness.

"She's creepy," Kieran whispered.

"What makes you say that? The weird voice? Or the way she kept staring at me?" I peered around me at the beautiful low-relief embossments and the expensive Turkish rugs covering the marble floor. The crystal candelabra above our heads held countless lit candles that threw a soft glow on the cherry wood furniture. A broad marble staircase led to a balustrade with a few doors I suspected were bedrooms. What impressed me the most, however, were the beautiful sculptural relief carved out of marble, from the railing to the ceiling and the borders adorning the furniture and doors. I inched closer and trailed a finger over what looked like tiny intricate flowers made of rose quartz adorning an incense holder carved from dark wood. They looked so fragile and yet so rich in detail, I wondered how any human being could possibly create something like this with their bare hands.

"It's Oriental," Aidan explained. "The Witches of Morganefaire are known for their craftsmanship in creating the most exquisite embellishments. They sell their brands for thousands of dollars. You wouldn't believe the waiting list for this stuff."

"It's not just merchandise they sell," Kieran whispered behind me.

I spun around and met his gaze. I had to admit I was very interested in what he had to say, but he clammed up when Aidan shot him his usual 'shut up' look.

"Let's get some rest. We'll have a long day ahead of us." Aidan touched my arm softly and kissed my neck. Even though I didn't appreciate his decisive tone, I let him guide me to the first bedroom, vowing to ask Kieran what he meant later. I didn't feel tired but I dropped on the thick brocade covers nonetheless, inhaling the softest whiff of crushed lavender as I figured I might as well close my eyes for a minute or two. When I woke up again, the sun was spilling through the high bay windows. I rubbed my temple to get rid of the heavy sensation inside my temples and brushed my hand over the covers to the empty spot next to me. Aidan's imprint was still there, but the space had cooled down, signaling he must've woken hours ago.

Sitting up, I looked around me. In broad daylight, the room looked spectacular with tall, white walls covered in embossed flowers and leaves that seemed to have a soft sparkle to them. The thick rugs I noticed upon our arrival felt as soft as melted butter under my naked feet. I took a moment to enjoy the tingly sensation, then slipped into clean clothes and headed out in search of Aidan.

I found him in the hall downstairs, engrossed in conversation with his brother, which ended the moment he saw me. I couldn't shake off the feeling they were hiding something.

"Good morning," Kieran said.

"Good morning. Am I interrupting?"

"No," Kieran answered. "You're like a glorious vision in that beautiful white dress."

I didn't want to point out that I was wearing jeans. Something was definitely wrong with him because his compliments were beginning to suck more than usual.

"Sleep well?" Aidan said, pecking my cheek. He smelled of lavender and honey, of home and hope that, now that we had arrived in Morganefaire, everything would turn out all right.

"Like a baby. I haven't slept that well in ages." I smiled and wrapped my arms around him.

"You look stunning," he whispered against my neck, his soft breath making my skin tingle. My heart began to race. "Are you ready to leave? We're being expected at the Council Court."

"Let me grab my purse and then I'll be ready to go." I broke our embrace and turned to head up the staircase, my mind already searching through the wardrobe for the right outfit to meet the Council when Aidan reached out to stop me.

"Please, Amber, don't sneak back into the bathroom or change your clothes again because we'll be late."

"That's so unfair," I said. "I bet you two had enough time to prepare."

Kieran frowned but didn't comment. I could sense he was worried about something, especially when he didn't have a sarcastic comeback. Besides, he took forever in the bathroom and was never ever finished before me, which led me to the conclusion they had used my absence to discuss matters they didn't want me to hear. There was definitely more to that conversation than they were letting on.

I swung my purse over my shoulder. "Don't worry, I wouldn't dream of making a bad impression."

"Thank you...for not arguing more than necessary." I could hear the relief in Aidan's voice, which pissed me off a little. He made me sound horribly argumentative, which I wasn't. I swear.

Chapter 4

The sun stood high on the horizon, bathing the medieval streets in glaring brightness. Even though it couldn't be later than nine a.m., Morganefaire's inhabitants were gathered on the narrow streets, going about their daily business, paying us no attention as we walked past. They were streaming toward what I assumed was the main business area, all of them witches and warlocks, all of them carrying Morganefaire's magic inside their blood. It was a melting pot of origins, of ages and sizes, but not necessarily of fashion. After seeing our guest quarters, I don't know what I expected. Maybe white wigs and the embroidered satin corsets of seventeenth-century France, or black robes and lots of pentagrams that screamed magic. What I saw, however, was mostly our century's trademark: blue jeans and cotton shirts, sprinkled with the odd flowing, oriental dress. I couldn't help but feel a little disappointed. Had I seen any of them walking down London's High Streets, I would never have guessed they were involved with the paranormal world.

Aidan seemed to know the way well for he navigated through the crowds at a hasty pace, only stopping here and there to utter a greeting or shake a hand. As I followed after him, I tried to ignore the sudden pang of hunger in my stomach and the burning sensation on my skin. Even though Kieran turned me after the Shadow ritual was performed, the spell was not fully passed onto me. Or maybe it malfunctioned because recently I had begun to suffer from bloodlust and now the sun was slowly starting to burn my skin.

"Are you okay?" Aidan whispered, sensing my thoughts.

Gritting my teeth, I nodded. "I'm fine."

"You shouldn't be out here in the sun until we figure out exactly what's going on."

"I'll buy a long sleeve shirt or something because I swear I'm not going back," I said.

"Let's check out the booths," Kieran said. "One's bound to sell clothing."

I rolled my eyes. Why were they so protective? "It's not like we're going to be in the sun all day."

"Yeah. Maybe a sweater or a shawl," Aidan said to his brother, ignoring me.

I shook my head grimly and pointed at the crowd ahead, wishing I had never told him because since I did Aidan couldn't stop worrying. "There's no time," I said. "Please, let's get this over and done with."

"As you wish." His remark was hesitant. There was defiance in his stance, as though he didn't want to honor my wish but couldn't bear upsetting me. I hated being treated like I had some deadly illness—or worse—like a damsel in distress that needed constant attention and rescuing.

"He'll get used to it," Kieran whispered in my ear. I shot him a thankful look even though I knew Kieran was wrong. Aidan always cared. It was part of his charm and one of the reasons why I fell for him in the first place. He would never stop worrying about anyone who mattered to him, which made us all weak spots in his otherwise perfect armor. I had to get rid of this bloodlust or else I might just prove the vampires' downfall.

A strong, burning sensation made me gasp. I looked down at the blisters forming on my arm. Kieran followed my line of vision. I pressed a finger against my lips, signaling him to be quiet, then hid my arm behind my back. He grimaced but kept my secret.

Nudging me, he whispered, "You need sunscreen. SPF 50+. I've heard that's the strongest out there. I'll get you some, okay?"

"Whatever." Even though I didn't want to acknowledge it, his concern touched me. Slowly I was becoming a part of their family.

"In here," Aidan said after what felt like an eternity walking in the burning sun. "Are you two coming?"

I smiled weakly and rubbed a hand over my forehead out of habit rather than to wipe off any sweat as we crossed an open space lined with marble pillars. He led us through a broad gate into a large hall with granite floors and yet more pillars. The air smelled of stale lavender incense and something else. I sniffed and almost gagged when the telltale craving hit me.

Blood. And lots of it.

What the heck were they doing in here? Opening up a slaughterhouse?

"Are you all right?" Aidan asked, steadying me. I felt Kieran's hand holding my arm, as though he, too, worried that I might just collapse into a messy heap.

"There's—everywhere." I choked on the word 'blood', unable to speak it out loud because of the power it held over me. My thirst was getting stronger by the day. If I didn't figure out how to stop it soon, I might just turn into a raging lunatic...or worse, start doing what Aidan and Kieran had been doing before undergoing the Shadow ritual: raid the local blood bank. I had fed a few times—mostly from myself—and it wasn't pretty. As much as my stomach grumbled, the thought of ever drinking blood again sickened me to the core. It was disgusting and yet delicious. Bitter and yet sweet. Those contradictions messed with my head. I mean, how could something so terrible be so addicting?

Kieran exchanged worried looks with Aidan. His eyes shifted uneasily a few times, communicating in that weird siblings way they must've perfected over hundreds of years. After a few moments of silence, Aidan's mouth turned into a grim line.

"Stay here with Kieran," he whispered in my ear. "I'm going in alone."

"Oh, no, you're not," Kieran said. "I didn't sign up to play babysitter. This is my fight just as much as it is yours."

I raised my chin a notch. "Nobody's babysitting me because I'm coming as well. And since I'm a vampire, this is my fight, too."

Kieran met my gaze. "I'm with her on this one."

Aidan hesitated.

"I'm not staying behind." I shook my head vehemently, just in case he wouldn't pay attention to my words. "I'm a vampire and I'll fight for my people. Well, half of them 'cause the other half's bad—" I waved my hand expressively "—you get my drift. Anyway, I have every right to be in there."

His stance hardened. "We don't have time for this."

"In which case stop just standing there and wasting away a perfectly fine day." I smiled and marched past him, praying I wouldn't make a fool of myself by walking in the wrong direction or getting lost in the vast corridors. Getting constant chuckles out of everyone around me wouldn't exactly aid my plight to be taken seriously in the paranormal world.

Chapter 5

To my delight, my sense of direction didn't forsake me. After a few turns, I found the Council room. Granted, I sort of followed the gathering mass spilling through the vast corridors framed by yet more marble pillars and carvings, but it still counts. The way I saw it, the word 'council' equaled a huge audience, meaning all those people were probably heading the same way as I was. Or so I hoped. For all I knew about Morganefaire, the council might as well hide in their medieval towers and communicate via carrier pigeons.

As soon as I reached the heavy mahogany double doors, I felt Aidan's hand on my shoulder. I turned and shot him a sideway glance. "Finally managed to keep up with me?"

"Not quite but I definitely tried." A radiant grin lit up his face and for a moment it even managed to erase his worry lines.

"See? I didn't wither in the sun," I said. Although I had to admit it felt like it when the scorching sun hit my exposed skin. Even though I would've loved to dive my arms in a bucket of ice, I played hardball. "I'm not the delicate daffodil you sometimes seem to think I am."

"Of course not." Aidan leaned into me and perched a quick but hot kiss on my lips, and my heart almost stopped in my chest. My mind made another entry in my personal mental diary, next to the many other entries marking various anniversaries. First meeting, first time holding hands, first date, first kiss, first time he said he liked me, then the other big L word, which made me want to declare my undying devotion to him for all of eternity. And now our first public kiss. I almost squealed with delight.

"Would you like me to bind you to a lamppost before you take off into the vast heights of the morning sky?" Kieran whispered behind me.

I signaled Aidan I'd stay close behind as he greeted some acquaintance, then whispered to Kieran, "Is it that obvious?" Amusement flared in his blue eyes and quirked the edges of his lips. There was my answer then. I frowned. Damn. My plan of keeping it cool and easy breezy light for the sake of staying interesting was flying right out the window. "Do you think I should tone it down a bit?" I asked. Kieran laughed. I narrowed my gaze. "What's so funny?"

He wiped a fake tear from his eye. His laughter stopped abruptly at my menacing expression, and he cleared his throat. "I remember a time when Aidan asked me the same question, that's all."

My heart fluttered in my chest. "Really?" A sense of pure love washed over me. I still couldn't get rid of the fear that my boyfriend might not be *that* into me. I mean, gorgeous vampire guy, perfect in every sense, falling for a chubby girl who lacked his sophistication, life experience, and knowledge of the world. It was hard to believe we shared an eternal bond. I still pinched myself every now and then, just to make sure it wasn't just a dream. Kieran's information definitely helped. I opened my mouth to beg for details when Aidan appeared at my side.

"Are you coming?"

His gaze wandered from me to Kieran and lingered there a tad too long. Something shifted in his expression: an unspoken warning, but that was about all I could pick up through our bond. Kieran smirked and walked past, ignoring him. Aidan grabbed my elbow and guided me inside. Unlike my usual self, I kept quiet because something else drew my immediate attention. As soon as we stepped through the doors, the blood scent became so intoxicating it made me choke on my breath. I clenched my hands until my fingernails cut through the barrier of my skin, and willed myself to gather my composure before I turned into a raging lunatic right there and then. But I knew I had to get this over with fast if I wanted to avoid the inevitable.

***

We came to a halt in a big round hall with more marble pillars and stone carvings. In the middle of the high ceiling was a glass ornament in the form of a hexagon that captured the light in a million facets and reflected it in a strong beam in the shape of a single bright star across the marble floor. Witches and warlocks were gathered to the east and west of the star. Their gazes were averted, but I could feel they were watching us. Waiting. Wondering. In front of us was a raised podium with a few seats. For the Council, I gathered, but the seats were empty.

"We're here. So what happens now?" I whispered to Aidan, pointing at the vast hall filled with people.

"We need to be officially seen and greeted," Kieran explained through gritted teeth. "It's all a terribly formal, meaning boring, custom. A bit like assessing an opponent in an open field, with lots of prancing up and down to figure out all his strengths and weaknesses, and trying to intimidate him along the way."

"Interesting." I glanced around, not really getting it. "So, exactly who is *on* the Council?"

"They're not here," Aidan said.

"But we're *in* the Council room at the designated meeting spot." I wondered why we were called to the Council room when there would be no council.

Aidan leaned closer to whisper, "The Council is a private organization made up of some of the most powerful people in Morganefaire. We're not allowed in without an invitation."

"Ah, I got it." I rolled my eyes inwardly. So, we were here to fluff our feathers like a glorious peacock and make a good impression. *If* we did our job well, then we *might* be allowed to meet the big wigs.

"This is the finest pretentious crap you'll ever see," Kieran said. I peered at his amused face, unsure whether he was being serious, or making fun of the gathering. Either way, for once I had to agree with him.

"Aidan McAllister and his companions have arrived," someone said. The room fell instantly silent. Countless eyes fell on us. I could feel their prodding gazes on my back, brushing over my skin.

"We're happy to have you back, brother," a towering, blond guy said, inching forward.

Aidan took his hand and gave it a vigorous shake. "It's good to see you again, Logan."

Logan greeted Kieran, then turned to me. "And this is your lovely lady?" His hazel eyes narrowed in a scrutinizing look. Surprisingly, he seemed quite young, around twenty or twenty-five. I wondered why he called himself one of Aidan's brethren when he was barely older than me. Maybe *Botox*, I figured, until he smiled and fine lines creased the thin skin around his eyes.

I returned the smile. "I'm Amber."

"A beautiful name," he said. "It suits you."

Heat rushed to my cheeks. "Thank you," I whispered, not sure what else to say.

"Your brethren have been expecting you," another male voice said. My attention snapped to the man standing to my right: just as tall as Logan, but at least ten years older with black curls, and more poise in his demeanor.

He walked over to Aidan and bowed this head slightly while making a strange gesture with his hands. "Merry Meet, and may the three Gods bless you with honor, strength and truth."

"*This* is one of the kickass Council guys," Kieran whispered. "It seems like they might honor us with their presence after all."

"Riley," Aidan greeted him. They exchanged a few words but my attention was already elsewhere engaged. Behind Riley stepped someone I immediately recognized.

Chapter 6

"Hi, Blake," I said, taking in the tan skin and dark hair that brushed the collar of what looked like an old-fashioned waistcoat stretched over his broad chest. Even though the large room wasn't fully illuminated, the pendant—a sapphire eye inside a triangle—dangling from a golden chain around his neck, shined unnaturally bright, almost as bright as the bronze flecks shimmering in Blake's burnished gaze. I swallowed hard at the memory of the same dark eyes focused on me when he tried to kill me only a few weeks previously in the hope to stop the Prophecy of Morganefaire. Aidan let him live, but only if Blake never came near me again. And then Blake saved my life from a werewolf and Rebecca's ghost, and asked me to bring Aidan to his brethren. He was once Aidan's best friend so, naturally, I had forgiven him a long time ago, but my boyfriend hadn't.

Aidan froze to the spot. Someone cleared their throat and then the room fell silent again. I knew Aidan wouldn't greet Blake over a cup of coffee and muffins, but his icy stance and lack of willingness to acknowledge him *at all* took me by surprise. Aidan's eyes swept over everyone but Blake, as though he wasn't standing only a few feet away from us. I wondered what would happen if someone locked them up in a tiny room, alone and with no means for escape. Would Aidan's Scottish temper boil over? Or would they kiss and make up like normal people?

Blake took a step forward, then stopped in his tracks, his gaze shifting from me to Aidan, then back to me. "I'm glad you could come," he said to no one in particular.

I elbowed Aidan in the ribs. He didn't budge, so I shot Kieran an imploring look and noticed his set jaw and the burning fire in his eyes. The McAllister brothers might bicker over every minuscule decision in their lives, but they sure knew how to stick together when it mattered.

I heaved an exaggerated sigh and nodded. "We're happy to see you."

"Speak for yourself," Aidan muttered under his breath.

"Why, where are my manners?" I continued unfazed, hopeful the McAllister brothers would get the hint. They didn't. "I just realized I have yet to thank you for your hospitality."

"I gather the accommodation is to your liking?" Blake said.

"Very much so. Thank you." I smiled and raised my brows at Aidan. He just frowned back. That was about all the small talk I could make. If he didn't take it from here soon, we'd end up with that uncomfortable silence that makes everyone start counting the seconds until it might be polite enough to get up and leave. I didn't get guys. Why couldn't they just put their primitive, alpha male battle on hold for a while and get on with whatever business they had with each other? Surely stopping the war was more important than mending their bruised egos?

Biting my lip, I tapped my fingers against my thigh and begged my mind to come up with something to say as my gaze shifted from one face to another. That's when I smelled blood again. I peered at the podium, only now realizing it wasn't a podium at all, but much larger—just like an altar, only with chairs set up around it. A few people had inched closer but didn't sit down. They stood as still as statues, watching us like you'd watch a theatrical performance, their faces mirroring their curiosity. I wondered how much they knew about us, about the war and the prophecy.

A sudden sense of vertigo made my head spin. My vision blurred and for a moment I thought I might just pass out on the marble floor. I forced myself to take shallow breaths, but the unmistakable scent of iron and copper coming from the altar hit my nostrils nonetheless, and a sense of dread washed over me. My brain screamed that I needed to get away from this place, and yet my feet remained firmly planted onto the ground. Running wasn't my style. Besides, my boyfriend needed my support. Okay, he didn't exactly say those words, but he told me in the past how much he needed me. I believed him and would grant him my undying loyalty and support until the very end of time because, deep down, I knew he'd do the same for me.

People wanted me dead, which made me conclude my necromancer abilities posed a great danger to Aidan's enemies. As of yet, I had no idea why because, surely, mediums and psychics could also talk with the dead. But as soon as I found out what those abilities entailed and why they were so special, I'd end up being of great help to Aidan and his brethren, or so my reasoning said.

Clearing my throat, I focused my attention back to the hall and Morganefaire's residents, realizing someone had yet to break the silence. As much as I hated being the center of attention, someone had to do it. Besides, with the scent of blood lingering in the air, I had to focus my attention on something more irrelevant.

"I like your style," I said, pointing at Blake's black waistcoat that made him look like an aristocratic undertaker from the Middle Ages with its medieval cut and the shiny material. I squinted, hoping it looked like genuine interest rather than a feeble attempt to avoid being blinded by the thing. "Is that satin?"

"Silk," Blake corrected.

"Easy mistake," I said. "They both originated in China, right?"

Blake hesitated, considering his words. "Yes, but silk is *natural* and satin is artificial. Silk is made from cocoons of silk worms and woven into clothes. A single strand of thread requires thousands of silk worms, which makes it more expensive and durable than satin."

I nodded again. "Maybe your designer can make me a dress." Not in a million years. "It would go well with—" I waved my hand, searching for words that seemed to have deserted me completely.

"You're a horrible liar," Kieran whispered behind me. In spite of the tense situation, his voice oozed with humor. I could've slapped the moron for having a laugh at my expense when I was doing all the hard work.

"So, who's your designer? I'm dying to know," I asked Blake, ignoring Kieran.

"The dumpster," Kieran muttered to Aidan, who seemed to want to stare a hole into the floor. Something went off inside me. I didn't know what was worse: Kieran's preschooler behavior, Aidan's arrogance and pride, Blake's talk about irrelevant things such as worms, or the smell of blood that just wouldn't stop torturing me. Whatever it was, I just couldn't bear it anymore. Didn't want to. I turned sharply and shot Kieran and Aidan irritated looks, then grabbed their arms and forced them a step forward toward Blake, until we stood in a close circle. "Okay, I get it," I hissed probably sounding like a lunatic. "Everyone's mad at everyone else. Aidan at Blake because he tried to kill me. And Kieran—" I pointed at him "—because you feel the need for a rare display of brotherly loyalty. And you, Blake, I don't know you long enough to know your motives, but I guess Aidan and you are even now that you saved my life. A life for a life. So let's be friends again, and get this over and done with."

"We're not even. He betrayed my trust," Aidan growled.

"I was protecting my best friend," Blake said through gritted teeth.

A dangerous glint appeared in Aidan's blue gaze. "You call killing my mate *protection*? You know exactly what happens to those who lose their bonded mates. Just look at Clare. It's not friendship if you wished that fate upon me." He took a menacing step forward until he stood mere inches from Blake. They were about the same size, towering over everyone else. Their gazes were locked in an intense stare, Aidan's filled with hate, Blake's mirroring something I couldn't quite pinpoint.

"How could I have known she was your mate?" Blake said. "It's not like you talked about your feelings for her. You told us she won the price and that we needed to free her from it."

Blake was definitely digging himself an early grave. Or would his insolence help? Silence ensued and for a moment I almost dared a smile, proud of myself that I got them to talk to each other...until Aidan said, "A true friend would've known. I should've let you rot when I had the chance."

"I proved myself to you time and time again," Blake whispered.

"The blood of a traitor is worth nothing to me," Aidan hissed. As if on cue, Kieran placed his hand on my shoulder, probably to prevent me from intervening. I shot him an easygoing smile to signal I wasn't planning to because, deep down, I believe that whenever a problem persists, people have to talk it out like adults. I was confident they shared my attitude...until Aidan's right hand wandered to his back where the sheath of his blade was usually located. Maya had removed our weapons, so I still wasn't worried. And then something silvery caught the light, making me realize Maya might not have found all of Aidan's weapons after all.

Aidan pulled out a blade, intent to use it. My stomach turned with fear and my heart began to hammer in my chest. The thought of a battle between life and death, of losing Aidan or seeing Blake harmed, froze me to the spot. The cave of my mouth became dry as pictures of blood covering the floor and walls invaded my mind. A low growl formed deep within my chest. My breathing quickened. I wanted to yell at Aidan to put the dagger away before it was too late, but the sound didn't find its way out of my throat.

Somewhere to my right, a door opened and closed with a loud thud. A man forced his way through the gathered crowd and inched closer. Through the blood fog before my eyes, I noticed the black, leather armor protecting his chest and the metal spikes adorning his worn boots.

He took a deep bow before Blake, then stopped in front of Riley, ignoring us. "Iain of the Night Guard," he said in a deep, guttural voice with an accent I couldn't place. "A girl has been found. I ask for permission to stain the hallowed ground."

"You may," Riley said.

Aidan's expression clouded. The tiniest bit of disappointment crossed his features as he slid the dagger back inside the sheath. I couldn't believe the guy. Did he really want to harm his former best friend? Any distraction was welcome now. I let out a sigh of relief and craned my neck to follow Iain through the crowd, out of the hall and then back in. Another man dressed in the same attire including the spike boots walked close behind, his strong arms carrying the small bundle of a teenage girl. Her long, golden brown hair brushed the floor as he placed her by Blake's feet, then stepped back and lowered his head, his hand clutching what looked like a silver sword fastened to his left hip.

The crowd gasped but didn't dare inch closer. A murmur echoed from the enclosed walls and turned into a penetrating buzz that grew in intensity. My heart pumped harder, faster, until I thought my chest might explode any minute. I covered my ears and forced myself to hold in my breath so I wouldn't inhale the copper scent that spread through the air like a blanket as I peered at the lifeless girl, ignoring the gathering crowd around me.

Her slightly chubby face, milky complexion and pink lips made her very pretty. Blake kneeled next to the motionless body and brushed her hair away from her face and neck, revealing unbroken skin. His hand moved to the nape of her neck, testing it, then down the contours of her body clad in a loose, green dress that reached down to her naked ankles.

"Whatever happened to her, it must've happened last night while she was asleep," I said. For the first time the witches and warlocks on the east and west side turned to regard me directly.

"Why?" Kieran whispered.

"Because she's still wearing her nightgown," Blake said grimly, echoing my thoughts.

"What do you think happened to her?" someone whispered.

The room began to spin. I blinked several times to get rid of the dizziness forming before my eyes, but it didn't work.

"It's hard to say," Aidan said. "There's no bruising. No blood."

"So, she died of a natural cause?" Hope oozed from Iain's voice. I peered from him to Aidan and knew instantly my boyfriend wasn't convinced.

"Could be," he said. "Except that the Prophecy of Morganefaire starts with someone's death. For all we know it could be hers."

"Yes, that's what the Seer saw, but the prophecy does not begin with the death of an ordinary witch," Blake said, his black eyes cutting into Aidan's, imploring him to keep quiet. "The verdict is she died of a natural cause. Iain, take her to the mortuary."

"The Council shall meet at a more appropriate time," Riley said. "Close the gates. No one's allowed in or out until the investigation concludes."

My gaze swept over the girl's chubby cheeks that didn't quite fit her otherwise thin body. I frowned and dared a quick sniff. Even though there was no sign of blood on her body, the telltale scent of copper hit my nostrils again.

"Please, something's wrong," a thin female voice echoed in my ear. "Something bad happened."

"Did you hear that?" I whispered to Kieran. I glanced around but only saw men standing nearby. He shook his head, wide-eyed. His gaze swept over the hall, unsure what to look for. I was obviously freaking him out again.

"Can no one sense it?" the thin voice asked again, making me shiver. The people around us kept staring at the girl's body, whispering to each other, but no one seemed to react to the voice. A ghostly presence? Maybe the spirit was calling out to me from the grave because she needed help.

My fingers hovered inches away from the girl's parted lips, and that's when it dawned on me. The scent came from inside her mouth. She might not have struggled because something or someone pinned her down, but she had bitten her tongue until she drew blood. Maybe Aidan and Kieran couldn't smell it because they didn't need blood to survive. Blake and I had never really been close so, for all I knew, he might just not have particularly good senses.

Kieran pulled me away and whispered in my ear, "What are you doing? We're trying to make a good impression here, remember? You can't touch a body with that facial expression. You look like you're starving."

"I'm sorry. I couldn't help it. I had to take a closer look."

"Why?"

My gaze sliced into his. "Because I think Aidan's right that she was murdered."

A moment later, Iain lifted the girl's body in his arms and carried her away.

"Please, I need to find out what happened," the female voice said. I turned slowly, careful not to draw attention to myself, and scanned the empty space around me. Nothing there. It irritated the hell out of me that I couldn't put a face to the voice. It made me feel like I suffered from a mental disorder.

Schizophrenia maybe, or multiple personality. If I didn't get out now and found an answer as to what was going on, I might as well check myself into a psychiatric ward.

"I need fresh air," I whispered to Aidan.

He shot me a concerned look. "I'll come with you."

I shook my head. "No, you stay here and finish up. I'll meet you in the hall outside, near the entrance." Faking a faint smile, I squeezed his hand and hurried out before he insisted on accompanying me. Ignoring the curious stares, I dashed through the crowds of people, following the scent of iron and copper down a flight of stairs to an underground vault and a closed, mahogany door. With a fleeting look over my shoulder, I pushed it open and entered the morgue.

Chapter 7

A voice had spoken to me—I hadn't been imagining things—and apparently I needed to find out what happened. I needed more clues and if sneaking into the morgue was what I had to do, then so be it. My body shook...and it wasn't because lifeless limbs scared me. Part of me feared visiting a place where resident souls still lingered near their bodies, screaming for help to come back to life or to have their requests fulfilled. With a gift like talking to the dead, every spirit would be attracted to me like a moth to a flame, but I'd still take the chance because living with a voice inside my head was out of the question. So I vowed to enter the morgue, inspect the body, and then get the heck out of there. And if I stumbled across a gathering of souls, I swore to myself I'd act as though I couldn't see them and make a beehive for the nearest exit. Sounded simple enough.

Unfortunately, the simplest things aren't always as easy as they seem.

The windowless room was about as big as a small chapel, and cold as ice. A couple of torches and candles burned bright, casting golden shadows across the cracked, white walls. The girl was spread out on a marble altar, a decorated slab with images of the sun and moon set up in the middle of the room. An inscription in fancy cursive was carved out in gold. The golden brown girl's hair was arranged around her like a halo; her long flowing dress brushed the stone floor. She looked so serene, as though she was barely asleep and would wake up very soon. It was hard to believe someone this young and pretty was gone forever.

Hesitating, I inched closer until my hand almost touched her cold skin. My fingers brushed over her mouth, then pressed lightly to part her lips and inspect the inside of her cheeks. Her jaw remained clenched tight. Rigor mortis, the rigidity that commences shortly after death, had already kicked in, meaning her limbs could no longer be bent without using force for at least a few more hours after which they would soften again. But I couldn't wait that long. To prove my theory that she had been awake during her attack and bit her tongue in fear, I had to peek inside her mouth and break a few bones in the process. The prospect of hurting someone—even someone already dead—horrified me. It just seemed wrong. Besides, for all I knew, the girl's ghost might still be hovering around this place. I had been to the Otherworld and knew ghost experienced their last moments and the brief period afterwards over and over again. The violation of her mortal carcass wasn't a memory I wanted to give her for all eternity.

I circled the altar once, then again, pondering my options, when the air above the girl's chest sparkled for a brief second. It could've been a trick of the candlelight or the figment of my imagination, and yet it made me stop on the spot. My gaze narrowed as I peered from her chest to the ceiling, then back down to her unmoving body.

The thin, golden thread was there, faint and barely noticeable, but there nonetheless. Frowning, I edged closer and bent forward until my face hovered inches away from the sparkling air. I had seen it before, when one of my friends, the devil's daughter Cass, almost lost her bonded mate and became a reaper. She had told me about the golden thread—the life cord, as she called it—that binds a human's soul to a mortal body and that it needed to be cut within hours upon one's death. The girl had been dead for at least a few hours, and yet no reaper had arrived to cut the life cord. I wondered why.

I watched the golden thread in silence. Maybe the reaper was late. Maybe her death had gone unnoticed in the Otherworld. Maybe something had happened to the designated reaper, which was unlikely but not entirely impossible. I don't know how long I just stood there, lost in thought, unaware of the entity watching me. A freezing sensation washed over me, but I attributed it to an uneasiness stemming from being in a room with a corpse. Eventually, I peered at one of the flickering candles, and that's when I saw the girl's ghost standing near the wall, her frightened gaze fixed on the altar. My mouth turned dry, my pulse spiked. The usual sense of fear and dread grabbed hold of me, but after my recent encounters with ghosts, both of the good and the bad kind, I knew running wouldn't get me far.

As though she felt my thoughts, the girl's hazel eyes shifted to me and our gazes connected. Her face remained blank for a second, and then she seemed to understand that I could see her. A tiny gasp escaped her chest, in shock, in surprise, I couldn't tell but the usual countless questions began to burn in her eyes. She wanted to understand what happened to her so badly, and yet how can you explain Fate?

"I'm sorry," I whispered, knowing too well my words wouldn't be able to offer consolation.

"You can hear me?" she asked. Her voice was thin and frail.

I nodded. "Someone will be here soon. They'll help you," I said, talking about the reaper. I didn't tell her the one coming would be a winged demon that would take her to either Heaven or Hell, depending on the kind of physical life she had led.

She shook her head. "*Someone?* You mean a demon from the pits of Hell?" She floated closer until she stood inches away from me. So the reaper had been here? Why hadn't he taken her soul? As if sensing my questions she continued, "Yeah, I nearly fainted when I saw it. The thing said I needed to stay a while longer. That I hadn't yet fulfilled my purpose. I don't even know what that means."

I blinked several times, confused. "Are you sure? Usually–" My voice trailed off as she nodded. Maybe her purpose was to tell us what happened to her. Even though I knew it was insensitive of me to ask about the last moments before her death, I figured I had no choice if I wanted to find out the truth and maybe even help her fulfill her purpose at the same time so she could move on. "Do you remember what happened to you?" I asked straight-out.

She seemed to consider my question for a moment, and then shook her head, wide-eyed. "It was night and I went to bed, as usual. Something woke me up, or maybe it was just a dream, I don't now. The next thing I remember is this room–" she clutched her chest as she took a deep breath "–and a demonic monster with black eyes and huge flapping wings. It commanded me in a deep voice to stay, and then it screeched making the walls vibrate, and it flew down through the stone floor right back into a lake of fire."

The lake of fire thing was definitely a figment of her imagination, but I kept quiet because the sight of a reaper would traumatize even the strongest and most boastful out there. It definitely wasn't for the faint of heart. Mind you, it made me want to run for my life the first time I saw one. "It's gone now," I said.

"There's nothing to fear." She nodded. "Do you remember anything else? Maybe about the night you—"

"Died?" She shook her head. Her eyes glazed over, as though she was about to cry. "Something felt wrong but it took me a while to realize I was dead. My first impression was that something happened since no one could see me. And then the demon arrived. Trust me, I spent the last hours trying to remember what happened. But it's all blank. I just don't understand why it had to happen to me." It was only natural to ask why she had to leave. They all felt their time had come too soon.

From what Cass told me, ghosts in the Otherworld recalled each and every gory detail about their death. That the girl didn't remember anything told me something was going on. I figured she might've suffered a concussion or something, so I asked, "What's your name?"

She didn't even blink as she answered. "Juliette Baron. My friends call me Julie." Her use of the present tense didn't go unnoticed. Even though she knew she was dead, she had yet to acknowledge the finiteness of it. I swallowed hard to get rid of the sudden lump in my throat.

"I'm Amber," I said with a weak smile. "Do you remember anything about your life, Julie?"

"What do you want to know?"

I considered my words. "For starters, who are your parents?"

"Like all the other children in Morganefaire, I've been brought up as an orphan and never met them."

My heart went out to her. "Maybe you can tell me where you live."

"I live in the house with the red brick wall in the south district of the city," Julie said, "around the corner from Elyssa's store." Her tongue flicked over her lips, leaving a sparkling trail of moisture behind. Her eyes narrowed for a brief second, as though lost in thought.

I wasn't familiar with the surroundings and made a mental note to ask Aidan who Elyssa was and where the south district was located, then moved on because I needed more clues. "Did you have a job?"

"Kind of." Her eyelashes cast a dark shadow on her cheeks as she lowered her gaze so I couldn't read her expression.

I raised an eyebrow. "Really?"

"The Blue Moon is about to hang low over Morganefaire, which happens rarely enough. But this time, it will stand in perfect alignment with four other planets. Because of the prophecy, the Council has decided to recruit for the Night Watch. I was supposed to join them in four days. When they chose me, it was a dream come true." Her eyes sparkled with passion and her chin tilted up with pride. Anger crossed her features a moment before she said, "I guess that won't happen now."

"I'm sorry." I averted my gaze and let my thoughts roam free for a moment. Seeing her so helpless made me feel like I had to do something—set her free, or whatever necromancers do. Basically, I had to find out the truth about her death. A concussion was highly unlikely because Julie remembered too much about her life. Besides, I smelled no blood on her head. So something else was the reason why she couldn't recall anything about the night she died. I needed to talk to Cass. She might know what could possibly be wrong with Julie's memory.

I straightened my back. Julie immediately turned to face me and her expression changed from sadness to worry. "Are you leaving? What if that monster comes back?"

"I need to talk to a friend," I said. "She might know more."

"Can I come with you?" She didn't wait for an answer, just inched closer, and I realized she was either a head taller than me, or floating above the ground. I peered at where her feet should've been and noticed thick, black fog reaching up to her calves, covering her skin.

"No, you need to stay here," I said, peeling my eyes from her feet—or lack thereof.

She frowned. "Why?"

"To watch the—" I pointed at her body.

"The table?"

"The—" *Body* I wanted to say but I couldn't bring myself to do it. I reconsidered my words. "In case someone pops in. Someone you might recognize." From the night she was killed, I wanted to add but didn't. "It might trigger your memory."

Julie's long hair spread around her like a curtain as she shook her head ever so gently. "But I don't understand. What am I supposed to watch?"

I sighed. She really didn't leave me any choice. "The body." Her confused expression told me she still had no idea what I was talking about. I pointed at the altar again. "*Your* body."

She looked from me to the altar then back to me. "I don't see a body." I peered away, uncomfortable. "Am I on the table?" Julie's ghost rose until she hovered in mid-air over the altar. "I am, aren't I?"

Even though Kieran was right in his claim that I was the worst liar ever, I shook my head vehemently. "My eyes are blurry from lack of sleep. Recently I was possessed and didn't even notice it. I'm new to this. A beginner, actually. Who knows if what I'm seeing is real anymore?"

"You're avoiding my answer." A hint of anger sparkled in Julie's eyes. "I don't know what happened to me, but I need your help to find out because you're the only person who can see me." There she said it and confirmed my suspicions. All spirits needed help, but I wasn't capable of helping her the way she imagined: taking her with me, answering her questions, helping understand. I had read about ghosts on the Internet, and how one request leads to another, one plead turns into the next. I wasn't ready to deal with the high demands of a ghost—not when my bloodlust and sensitivity to light could flare up any second.

"I can't," I said. "The best thing I can do is ask my friend for advice, then return to tell you what she said. I don't have the answers you seek. I don't know what purpose you're supposed to fulfill, and I sure can't start snooping around this place."

"No, you're the only person who sees me so you need to help me find out." She shook her head, wide-eyed, adding, "Please?" Her voice sounded whiny, pleading now, reminding me of an upset child.

I took a deep breath to help me stay resolute. "I want to, but I'm an outsider. Nobody will talk to me or take me seriously. Besides, I have no idea what to do." All I had wanted was to find some additional clues and then share them with Aidan, who seemed to doubt Blake's theory of a natural death, so I figured Aidan could take it from there. I never planned on meeting the girl's ghost. She should've been long gone. Having a ghost around me 24/7 wasn't an option, not least because a ghost's unpredictable. Julie might be a nice person one minute, and the next she could turn into a raging lunatic. I had seen it all before. Actually, not really, but I had *read* all about it in various forums and it scared the crap out of me. I didn't need to see it live to believe it.

Julie pressed her hands against her hips. "You can't just leave me here."

"Look, I understand you're upset because you're—" I stopped, realizing my blunder. Seriously, this tendency to pick all the wrong words was beginning to tick me off. I had to start thinking before I opened my mouth.

"Dead," Julie prompted, her eyes sparkling again.

"I didn't mean it like that."

"I'm not upset," she said, ignoring me. "I'm fuming mad. How could I have died days before joining the Night Guard?" Uh-uh, there it was: a ghost's inability to control her temper.

I sighed, wondering how long I had been in here and whether Aidan might already be looking for me, worrying his head off, as was his style. "Words cannot express how sorry I am, Julie. I promise I'll ask my friend, Cass, for advice. Until then—" I backed off toward the door, taking one small step at a time. Maybe she wouldn't notice if I just sneaked through. I felt horrible at the thought, and yet there was no other option. I vowed to ask around, and then come back and share my findings with her, after which I'd leave her to fulfill her purpose. Surely if the reaper wanted me to accompany her all the way, someone might have left me a note? Taking care of a ghost is a full-time job, minus the perks of actually being paid for it. I wasn't sure I had the time to solve a mystery with the vampires teetering on the brink of a war.

Besides, Aidan and I were in a new relationship and a ghost doesn't exactly know the notion of 'privacy'.

The door was only a step or two away now. I eyed the handle, then decided to dash for it when Julie bellowed, "Whoa, what are you doing? You're not leaving without me. Because I swear I'll haunt you for the rest of your life."

I turned sharply, my gaze throwing daggers. "You wouldn't!"

She raised her chin defiantly. "Try me. I might be new to this and not really know what I'm doing, but I'll figure it out. I mean, how hard can it be to make your neighbors' dogs howl half the night, slam a few doors and windows, and mess with electricity so you'll never ever get a good night's sleep again? I don't know if I ever told you but I'm a fast learner. Did you know I'm a witch? I could even cast a spell on you." Now, that was troublesome. She inched closer, and for a moment I thought she only wanted to threaten me or something, until she began blowing out one candle after another, bathing the room in semi-darkness.

"Enough," I said irritated as she reached the last two. "I got your point."

"Are you sure? Because I think I can do more freaky stuff. Watch my eyes." She turned to face me. I peered away, though I caught a glimpse of two white spots shining in the darkness from the corner of my eye. "Hey, you're not watching," she said, laughing.

"Creep," I muttered under my breath. The forum threads I had recently checked out popped back into my head. Sweet Julie was slowly but steadily turning into a poltergeist. Soon I might just have to start explaining to Aidan why we had scary noises inside our home—yet again. I felt like slapping myself for making the beginner's mistake of talking to her in the first place.

"I command you to stay here, or I'm calling a pastor to teach you some manners," I hissed.

She snorted. "Good luck with that. I know everyone in Morganefaire. Half of them barricade their doors at night in fear of what might be lurking in the shadows. And the other half would kick you out so no one associates them with a necromancer."

My jaw dropped. "How do you—"

"Know what you are?" She rolled her eyes, giving her angelic face a possessed flair. I took a step back, realizing she didn't look half as cute as I initially thought she did. "Please! I might be living in the Middle Ages, but I'm not stupid," Julie continued.

"Yeah," I muttered, "but I am." For ever venturing into a morgue and thinking everything would turn out all right. I was the biggest idiot on earth.

She glided closer, forcing me against the wall. "Where are we going first? Home to investigate whether someone saw something? That might be a good idea."

I shook my head. "My boyfriend's waiting upstairs."

"Can he help? Is he cute?" Her pale hand wrapped around the handle and yanked the door open with no effort at all. I gawked, unable to turn away. Blowing out a few candles was one thing; this was a whole new level. I was aware ghosts could do all sorts of things, but I never figured it was that easy. Julie started down the hall, calling over her shoulder, "Are you coming, or what?"

She took a left turn. Seeing my chance, I turned right and raced down the corridor in the hope I'd shake her off. I didn't even reach the next corner when she appeared in front of me with a furious glance.

I raised my hands defiantly. "Okay, got it. You want me to follow, so I'll just follow." Lost for words, I trailed after her, up the stairs and past the crowd of people. This time I paid no attention to their curious glances and their whispering. I had more important things on my mind, like my immediate need to get rid of a ghost.

"Amber!" Julie's voice echoed through the walls, startling me. My heart hammering hard in my chest, I peeked around the corner where she was standing next to Aidan and Kieran, the black fog around her feet hovering above the ground so she could be the same height as Aidan, her nose pressed against his. "Who is he? I've never seen him before, and I know everyone in Morganefaire."

"You said that already," I muttered. "And that would be my boyfriend."

She floated back, wide-eyed. "Oops, sorry. My mistake. Didn't know he was taken." She made it sound like we were talking about something as trivial as a chair. I sighed, thinking thank God she knew when to back off. And then she turned and her eyes focused on Aidan's brother. "Oh! I've just spotted someone even hotter. And he's closer to my age, too."

"I doubt that," I said. Kieran was hundreds of years old. The girl couldn't be older than eighteen, twenty tops.

"I want details," she squealed. "Who's the gorgeous hunk with the dark blue eyes and beautiful black hair standing next to the less hot one? If I was alive, I'd be so all over him."

"That'd be Kieran. My boyfriend's brother," I said, ignoring the fact she just called my boyfriend 'less hot.'

"Kieran." Her voice turned dreamily. "The name suits him."

Before I could answer, Aidan spied me and headed in our direction. "Where have you been?"

I moistened my lips and wrapped my hand around his upper arm, whispering, "I need to talk to you. Julie's ghost is here."

"Tell him I have the hots for his brother," Julie said, circling around Kieran as she regarded him up and down like you'd stare at a dress in a shop window.

"Who's Julie?" Aidan asked a tad too loudly.

"The ghost that wants to jump your brother's bones."

He raised his brows. "What?"

I pressed my finger against my lips. "Shhh. It's the girl that just died and she can hear you."

Aidan's gaze swept over the air and the floor. "Where is she?"

"Almost snogging Kieran's face off," I muttered, pulling him closer to me so no one would hear us. "Something happened to her and she won't leave me alone until we find out what. We need to talk, but not here."

Aidan nodded and motioned Kieran to follow us as we headed home with Julie still hovering in mid-air as she kept staring at her new flame, mesmerized by whatever poor, clueless Kieran seemed to exude.

Chapter 8

"A ghost has been bothering you and you haven't fainted yet?" I gritted my teeth as Kieran's voice boomed through the room, followed by his irritating laughter.

It was the same thing every time he remembered I was a necromancer. I was forced to listen to his shameless attempts at making fun of me simply because I had won the Prize of Sight in a crazy demi-goddess's paranormal race. Whether I wanted it or not, I was stuck with it for the next five hundred years. So, after a long period of denial followed by a longer period of being scared out of my mind at the prospect of ever meeting a ghost, I was struggling to accept my fate now. Kieran sure wasn't making this easy on me and I had no intention to keep my mouth shut until he'd get bored and leave me alone.

Grimacing, I punched him in the ribs a bit harder than intended. "I wish we could swap places just for a day. I doubt you'd do better than I did. Mind you, I bet you'd be running around like a headless chicken, screaming like a frightened little girl the way you do whenever you see one of Hell's gargoyles."

"Now you're being hurtful." He pressed a hand against his chest, as though my words hurt him indeed, but I knew his seriousness was fake. Kieran was the most easygoing person I had ever known. It usually took more than a lighthearted insult to upset him.

"Where did you even find her?" Aidan asked from the open backdoor, where he'd been standing for the last ten minutes, massaging his temples the way he always did when he thought it was all my fault.

I groaned and pushed my hair out of my eyes. At least he believed me now. Until a week ago I could barely get him to acknowledge the existence of ghosts. That's what denial does to you. "In the morgue. You said you didn't believe she died of a natural cause so, obviously, I went to investigate."

"Obviously," Aidan muttered.

I decided to ignore him as I continued. "She was alone and looked so scared, so I decided to talk to her."

"Alone and scared?" Julie huffed. "Well, you'd be, too, if you suddenly woke up in a morgue, talking to a demon that I thought wanted to tear through my flesh and gauge out my eyes."

I hushed her. She turned her back on me, annoyed.

Aidan opened his mouth to speak. I raised my hand to stop him. "Don't tell me. I know it was a stupid mistake. She must've taken my concern for an open invitation to haunt me."

"You gave me no choice," Julie muttered. "You help me, and after this is over you won't see me again. That's the deal. Take it or leave it." I sighed exasperated. It was a great deal...for her because, the way I saw it, I was drawing the shorter straw either way.

"At least you're not being possessed again," Kieran said, inching closer until he stood inches away from my face, his eyes scrutinizing me. "Or are you?" He turned to address Aidan. "Are you sure it's even her? Don't you think she looks a bit grumpier than usual?"

I rolled my eyes. "How people could stand living with you for five hundred years is beyond me."

"Whoa!" Julie gasped. "Five hundred years? Hot dude is a walking—What the hell is he?" Her forehead creased in concentration. She almost choked on her breath as she put two and two together. "He's an angel, isn't he?"

Kieran an angel? Seriously? I wanted to slap my forehead. Or hers. "He's a vampire, Julie."

"Oh." I could tell from her incredulous expression she didn't want to believe me. "But how can he walk around in daylight?"

I decided to ignore her because that's what people in the paranormal forums instruct one to do upon meeting a ghost. So far that advice proved useless, but I figured I could give it another try. I turned my attention back to Kieran and Aidan. "Let's talk about more important matters, like getting rid of Julie."

"Yeah, well, I want to hurry this deal up too," Julie said.

"You're freaking me out whenever you stare into thin air like there's someone there." Shuddering, Kieran put some space between us, as though I wasn't right in the head...and paced straight through Julie's ghost.

I regarded him intently, waiting for a reaction from him that he at least felt *something*. He slumped into the plush sofa and placed his booted feet on the side table, unaware of Julie's adoring stare.

"He's so cute, Amber," she said. "Did you notice how he tried to touch me?"

I shook my head. "He didn't."

"Oh, he so did." She peered at me triumphantly. "You're just jealous I got the hotter guy."

There, she said it again. I couldn't let this one slip by. "Julie, he doesn't even hear you."

"He's so pretty, he's so fine, I just wanna make him mine," she began to sing, over and over again. I wanted to press my palms against my ears to tune out the high-pitched noise. Not only did I manage to pick up an irritating ghost, but also one who was bordering on the cuckoo side.

"What's she doing?" Kieran asked.

"See? He senses me," she exclaimed in joy. The girl was definitely living in a fantasy world.

"You don't want to know," I mumbled.

"She's that bad, huh?" Aidan's gorgeous lips curved into the most stunning smile. I rose on my toes to kiss him but only managed to reach his chin. Good enough for me. "What happened to her?" he continued.

I shook my head. "Don't know. She can't remember, which is strange because it's about the only thing she can't recall. The reaper turned up but never cut the life cord. Apparently she's supposed to fulfill a purpose. She thinks it has something to do with her death, which is why she wants me to help." I clicked my tongue, remembering I completely forgot to address the incident in the hall, think Aidan drawing his dagger at Blake. Aidan probably thought his behavior was justified, meaning a discussion would turn into a confrontation. I wasn't up for it so I moved on to a more relevant matter. "Don't you think it's strange that something happened to Julie on the day of our arrival?"

"She died the evening *before* we arrived." Aidan inspected the corridor, then closed the backdoor leading to the garden and sat down on the sofa opposite from Kieran, drawing me close. It was his way to signal we were about to have a private conversation. A dark shadow crossed his features. He moistened his lips and shook his head slightly. "The girl was murdered, there's no doubt about it, and yet Blake insisted she died of a natural cause."

"It seems like he's trying to cover it up," I said.

"Are you sure you're not being paranoid again?" Kieran said with a smile, but his voice betrayed an edge that told me he trusted his brother's judgment. He set his feet down from the table and leaned forward, listening intently.

"I smelled blood on her," Aidan said.

I nodded. "Me too. It was the reason why I went to investigate her body in the first place. And that's when I met the ghost. People don't usually go around smelling of blood."

"Unless a girl has that time of the month." Kieran's voice trailed off, embarrassed.

I shook my head. "She must've bit her tongue during the attack, which brings me to the question why there were no marks or any sign of a struggle on her body."

Aidan took a deep breath and let it out slowly. A frown creased his forehead as he began to go through possible explanations. The moment he turned to face me I knew he had come up with a good one. "When you were possessed by Rebecca's ghost you did things she wanted you to do." I nodded, so he continued, "You said you had no choice. Do you think Julie was possessed and killed herself?"

I pondered his question for a few seconds. It was possible but not likely. Suicide usually leaves a trail behind, a last attempt to save oneself at the last minute, which I told him adding, "Unless it was odorless poison, in which case she could've died in her sleep and never noticed."

"She could've suffocated after taking it," Kieran chimed in.

"Suffocation's not likely. You would've seen small red or purple blotches in her eyes or on her face," Aidan said.

"Look who watched *Law And Order!*" Kieran winked at me.

I stifled a snort. "Nah, he wouldn't be caught dead switching on the television set. Being born in the middle ages, he probably thinks a talking box is the devil's invention straight from the pits of Hell."

"Thanks for making me feel old." Aidan grimaced and shot us an irritated look, his eyes sparkling. He looked so cute when he was wound up. I squeezed his hand.

"I say we get some swabs, skin cells, fingerprints, DNA, the whole shebang," Kieran said.

"If this place had forensics, we'd be golden." I heaved a sigh. "Until then you'll have to make do with my immortal eyes. Unfortunately, they saw nothing."

"An autopsy could pinpoint the exact cause of death," Kieran persisted.

"Cut me up?" Julie hissed in my ear. "I think not!"

"Do you know any medical examiners? I asked Kieran.

A pause, then, "Well, no."

I smiled. "Then shut up."

We fell silent again. A grandfather clock stroke a full hour, and then silence enveloped us once more. I realized even Julie had become quiet, meaning she was still listening to our conversation. As uncomfortable as that made me feel, I figured it might just kick-start her memory, so I didn't try to send her away. I removed imaginary lint from my jeans, avoiding her wide-eyed, questioning gaze.

Kieran spoke first. "Maybe it wasn't so much poison as something else that made her pliant."

"I didn't eat or drink anything out of the ordinary," Julie said quietly, her thin voice startling me. My gaze swept over her stubborn expression. "Every night, we have bread, butter and water, which is served in the community room. It would've been hard to poison me and not everyone else in the room."

I relayed her words to Aidan and Kieran.

Kieran cocked a brow. "Bread and butter? Where was she? Prison?"

"Focus," Aidan said sharply.

Kieran cleared his throat and tapped a hand against his thigh, thinking. ""So, it wasn't poison. Mind control, then. I really think she killed herself."

Julie gasped. Hearing other people talking about her death couldn't be easy, so I shot her a sympathetic look. "There's something I need to do. See you later," she said. Keeping her head high, she smiled weakly and floated past me through the closed door.

"Sure. Take your time," I whispered after her.

"Is she gone?" Aidan asked. I nodded. "Poor girl."

"I think the suicide part was a bit too much," I said, "and I couldn't agree more. We're not in *Star Trek*."

Aidan's jaw set. And that's when I remembered my first date with him. He was an immortal bounty hunter; I was a mortal unaware of the existence of his world so, naturally, I had been nervous, even scared because I somehow felt the danger around him. And although I was both physically and spiritually drawn to him, I had no intention to hook up with the boss. So what exactly happened to my resolution? I tried my best to resist his good looks, but then he did something to me. I'm pretty sure he invaded my mind to soothe me, sending me into a deep sleep, from which I only awoke when his lips pressed against mine in the most tender kiss I ever had. I shuddered at the thought, and it wasn't just with pleasure.

"Can a vampire influence your mind?" I asked, staring at Aidan directly in the hope he'd get the hint. He didn't and I made a mental note to ask him when we were alone in our bedroom. That is, if Julie had a sense of privacy.

"Not any vampire. Only the first or second generation after a master," Aidan said.

I did the math inside my head. "You're a second generation. Rebecca was a first since she turned you. And she was turned by—"

"Her master, Flavius," Aidan said.

"He's dead," Kieran whispered. "And Rebecca's a ghost."

Aidan hesitated, considering his words. "But they will rise. Once all four shards merge, the mirror can turn anyone into flesh and blood. That's what the prophecy's all about. Three races fighting for supremacy, of which the vampires could be the winners. And by vampires I mean Flavius, Rebecca, and their army. They're about the last people you want to win a war." Aidan shut his eyes as he spoke, his memory traveling back. Because of our bond, pictures flooded my mind: pictures of pain and tears, of death and destruction washing over the world. I shook my head to get rid of the disturbing images but only managed to intensify them, until Aidan opened his eyes again. There was urgency in them. Whatever Rebecca's plans were, recent events had shown that she had come a lot closer to her goals when she found fragments of the mirror that could entrap souls and release those trapped. Aidan had one shard of the mirror, Rebecca the other three. I had no doubt she'd attack us to get her hands on the last fragment. And then her master would return to claim the world.

"That reminds me, did you get a meeting with the Council?" I asked Aidan.

He shook his head. "Blake's trying but it's as though they're avoiding us." He spat his former friend's name like it was poison.

I sighed. "I know you're still mad at him, but can you please try to put it all aside, at least until this war's won?"

He squirmed in his seat, hesitating, which made me groan. Aidan was as stubborn as a mule. Cass claimed it was a trait Scottish men are known for but, usually, he was also known for being the sensible one. That he wouldn't budge in this particular case made no sense.

"What's wrong?" I brushed his hair out of his eyes, ignoring Kieran's warning look.

Aidan turned to face me but didn't answer. His grim expression reflected the way he felt inside: torn, unsure what to do. I tuned into our bond and let my mind reach out to his, fighting layer of layer of emotional fog and secrecy, when the telltale barrier hit me with full force. He wasn't ready to share whatever bothered him.

"You're keeping secrets again," I said, pushing him away angrily.

"He's not the one keeping secrets," Kieran whispered. "It's Blake. So don't be angry at him."

I narrowed my gaze. "What secrets?"

"Secrets that can cost him his life," Kieran said.

"I don't understand. Whose life?" I asked, confused.

"Blake's," Kieran elucidated.

My thoughts began to race, putting two and two together. In my twisted reasoning, all I understood was that my boyfriend wanted to kill Blake for keeping secrets. I shot Aidan a glare. "And you're considering telling on him, maybe even killing him." I shook my head vehemently and yanked at his arm to get his attention. "No, Aidan, you can't do that. He was your best friend. If I can forgive and forget, then so can you."

He frowned, his expression brooding, intense. A shadow crossed his features a moment before he realized the meaning of my words. "What? No. Of course I'd never betray my brethren. An oath stays an oath. Kieran wasn't talking about me. We think someone found out Blake's secret, but they don't know how to prove their claims. So they might be trying to blame him for Julie's death to get rid of him."

My mind wandered back to everything I knew about Blake. I didn't get it. What secret could he possibly have that someone would want to frame him for a murder he didn't commit?

Aidan inched closer and whispered in my ear, "He's different." I raised my brows, signaling I still had no clue. "Do you remember when I told you I saved his life?" I nodded so Aidan continued, "Without me he'd be dead."

"Like in cold as a stone," Kieran chimed in.

I waved my hand about. "Yeah, I know Blake's a vampire."

Aidan cocked a brow meaningfully. "Yes, but his people don't know it."

Did he say *his* people? And that's when it dawned on me. Blake wasn't just a vampire, he was also a male witch: a warlock—and the people of Morganefaire had absolutely no idea about it. I shrugged. "So what's the deal? They've welcomed your kind for hundreds of years."

Aidan sighed. I couldn't tell whether from frustration or from the realization that I really had no idea about anything. He pulled me closer and wrapped his arms around me, whispering, "Remember our gates back home? They're infused with magic to keep out the Shadows." I nodded, unsure where this conversation was heading. He continued, "They contain witch's blood. But the witches and warlocks of Morganefaire stopped selling their blood hundreds of years ago. Blake let me use his own blood without their knowing, which makes him a traitor."

"Add the fact that he's one of us now when he's actually mentioned in the prophecy as Morganefaire's future leader, and that's a sure death sentence," Kieran said. "The Council will never allow a vampire warlock to lead them, and particularly not when it looks like the vampires planned the whole thing by turning Blake."

The gravity of his words sat in the pit of my stomach like a rock. "But no one can prove anything, right? It'd be his word against the other person's." The room fell silent for a moment as I tried to make sense of the chunk of information. One question remained unanswered though. "How come Blake's not sensitive to light, like Clare? The Shadow ritual wasn't performed on him." I thought back to our talk about silkworms. Silk was more light filtering than satin. Maybe he used it as a protective shield. It sounded far-fetched, but I couldn't dismiss the idea.

"That's right," Aidan said. "Since witch's blood courses through his veins, he only had to perform—"

"His own magic to get rid of it," I finished, finally understanding.

"There's still some sensibility, which is why he wears thick clothing," Aidan said. "Witches and warlocks are mortal; Blake isn't. But, unlike us, his wounds take longer to heal, and if they're vicious enough he could even die."

And that's when it dawned on me. "Is that why you pulled out your dagger and went all cuckoo for all people to see?" I whispered in disbelief.

Aidan nodded gravely. "The plan was to hurt him so everyone would see his wounds didn't heal instantly, which would've proved he wasn't a vampire." My jaw dropped.

Kieran laughed. "Did you really believe we'd kill him?"

I lowered my gaze, ashamed that I really thought Aidan was about to turn into a raging psycho. "So it was all show?" I asked, incredulous.

"Pretty much." Aidan's smile disappeared and his expression darkened again. "But that doesn't mean

Blake and I are friends again. That period of our lives is over."

Chapter 9

I was so absorbed in our conversation that I didn't even notice when Julie returned. Daylight had just given way to darkness when we finally stood from our seats on the sofa and went about closing the shutters for the night. According to Aidan, that wasn't so much a choice as expected of us in Morganefaire.

"You don't leave your curtains undrawn or shutters open, not if you don't want the Council talking sense into you," Kieran said. "And by talking I don't actually mean the use of words. More like ending up at the bottom of a cold, freezing lake tied to a giant slab of concrete."

"It's not so much their unwanted attention you should be worried about, but the fact that the night has countless ears," Aidan said dryly. "It'd rather not have them tune in to our conversation."

I nodded and finished up barricading the house, then returned to my place on the sofa. Aidan was already there, waiting for me. His arms wrapped around me like I always belonged in them. As his bonded mate, it was my rightful place by his side, and he wasn't afraid to show it at any given opportunity.

Breathing in his scent, I relaxed and almost forgot the world around me...until I felt Julie's gaze on me. Even though I should've been used to sensing ghosts by now, a cold shudder ran down my back. It wasn't malice that mirrored in her eyes, but it wasn't happiness for us either. And how could I blame her? When death came to claim her physical body, it also took with it any chance of finding love again.

Out of respect for the pain she must be going through, I put some space between Aidan and me, and cleared my throat.

Aidan frowned and his grip around my hand tightened. "What's wrong?"

"She's here, isn't she? That ghost chick, Julie," Kieran said, glancing around. "Where is she?"

A smile lit up Julie's face. She definitely had a crush on Kieran. I raised my chin slightly and pointed. "To the left by the table."

"She can listen in if she wants to," Kieran said. "Just make her stand by the window or something."

"Are you scared?" I teased.

"Well, it was different in a public place, but now we're all trapped in a room. You've got to admit that's a little freaky."

"Yeah, it's awkward with you two hanging around all the time," Julie said, pointing at Aidan and me. She inched closer until she hovered in mid-air inches away from Kieran, the black fog around her feet gathering around him like a cocoon. "Tell him I don't bite...unless he wants me to."

"She says she doesn't bite...unless you want her to." I smiled as Aidan rolled his eyes.

"You just don't get it, do you?" Kieran said. "I don't want her drooling all over me while I take a shower—naked. I demand a little privacy because, when women see me without my clothes on, well, let's just say they can't help themselves."

"You wish." I laughed. The sad thing about Kieran was that he really thought he was God's gift to the female population.

"I kid you not." Kieran sat up, wide-eyed, and shook his head. "Last time I was in London on bounty hunter business I had to check into a hotel. I didn't notice the open curtains—"

"You left them open on purpose," Aidan cut in.

Kieran continued, ignoring him. "Imagine me taking a shower when the phone rings—"

"I'd rather you didn't," Aidan whispered in my ear.

My lips twitched as I squeezed his hand to quiet him and tuned back into Kieran's sordid story.

"—so I hurry to answer it. She must've seen me naked from the opposite building because five minutes later there's a knock on my door and this chick basically throws herself at me."

I rolled my eyes and laughed. "I'm wondering how much of that story's true."

"All of it," Kieran said. "I'm like a magnet or something. One of a kind."

A glance at Julie's adoring stare told me she more than likely believed every word he said.

"Now that we've established Kieran's attractiveness," Aidan muttered, "we need to devise a plan to get Morganefaire's support. Solving Julie's murder might help us gain their trust."

"I say we include Blake, and then we can have a big party where everybody gets drunk and we can all bond," I said, not really meaning the last part. Aidan's hard stare made me shrug. "What? I know you're worried about his secret, but no one will be able to prove anything. Besides, we need allies. Without him, I'd be dead so that makes him no worse than anyone else out there."

Aidan nodded, seemingly considering my words. "Okay, but if he so much as lays a finger on you, he's dead."

Our fingers intertwined and he shot me a broad smile. I knew he meant his threat and was only trying to make it look like it was merely a joke so it wouldn't upset me. I wanted them to get along again because I knew how much it meant to both of them.

"The Blue Moon is in a couple days. We don't have time for solving Julie's murder, wasting our time negotiating with the Council, and preparing our brethren for war." Kieran leaned back against the sofa with a sigh. "If only there were five of me."

I peered from him to Julie who hovered next to him, her ghostly fingers brushing his dark hair, her eyes shining dreamily. She had to go—and pronto—because she kept distracting me. He was right, there were too many things to do. We had to split up. "I'll solve the mystery. You guys focus on the Council," I said. "I'll start with the people she grew up with, such as her parents. Maybe someone knows who'd kill her."

Aidan shook his head. "That's a dead end. Keeping the parents' identity a secret is a huge deal in Morganefaire. You're more likely to win the lottery."

"I didn't have any enemies," Julie said. "Everyone liked me."

"A jealous friend, maybe?" I asked her. She shook her head, wide-eyed.

"Right." I bit my lip, thinking of alternatives, and turned back to Aidan. "We could question who found her. They might've noticed something."

"I'm sure Blake did that already," he said. "That's about the first thing anyone would do."

"We need something else," Kieran said. "Anything to get us started at this point. Did she say anything to you?"

I bit my lower lip as I recalled my meeting with Julie. In the short time span, I barely got to ask a question. The only hint I had was that for some reason the reaper wouldn't cut the cord and transport her soul to the Otherworld. "I could call Cass and ask her about the whole reaper thing," I suggested.

Aidan hesitated. "You could," he said eventually, "but you know her. She's not interested in Hell's business. Even if she asked her father, I doubt Lucifer would share his secrets with us."

"Maybe Dallas could find out for us." After my brother almost died at Rebecca's hands, I didn't want to drag him into the whole affair, but he was Cass's bonded mate and Lucifer's future son-in-law. Maybe Lucifer had started to include him in Hell's business.

"Only as a last resort," Aidan said. "I couldn't watch your pain if something were to happen to him again."

"You're so sweet to think of my feelings. Thanks." I smiled and touched his cheek in the hope he could feel my love for him. Our gazes met and my whole being began to melt into his, becoming one.

"Hey, focus." Kieran's voice jerked me out of the moment. I broke away first but my gaze still lingered on my boyfriend. The top button of his shirt was unopened. I fought the strong urge to rub my fingers against the soft patch of pale skin that peered from beneath. When I raised my gaze, Julie was staring right at me, her eyes filled with a fire I had rarely seen in others. That's when a thought struck me and my breath almost caught in my throat.

"Do you know anything about the Night Guard?" I said.

"Why?" Aidan asked warily.

"Julie told me she was about to join it. She was recruited but died before she could commence her position."

"Why would they recruit a nineteen-year-old girl?" Aidan's expression changed from curiosity to mistrust, then to determination.

"I don't know. What are the Night Watch's tasks?" I asked her, interested. Kieran's brow furrowed. He still couldn't accept me seeing ghosts.

"They walk up and down the wall and watch over the city at night. Protect it. Warn the Council in case of an intruder," Julie said.

"Were you trained?"

She nodded. "Everyone is."

I tapped my fingers against my thigh, thinking. "So the task is to watch over the whole city, or just a certain part?"

"One district only," she said. "I don't know which district I would've received." I passed on the information to Aidan and Kieran.

"It sounds like someone didn't want her to become a night guard," I said. "Now we only need to find out why. Thanks, Julie." I shot her a smile.

"You've definitely given us our first vital clue about why she might've died." Aidan's lips twitched. "You are the smartest—"

"Most determined," I added.

"Yes, that too." His lips curled up into a lazy smile and a tiny dimple appeared in his cheek. My fingers itched to touch it. "Don't forget trustworthy."

Julie pretended to stick her finger down her throat. "I'm going to puke."

I ignored her and batted my eyelashes at my sexy boyfriend who planted a soft kiss on my lips. "You're forgetting an important one," he said. His finger trailed down my neck. Heat flooded through my body.

"What's that?" I whispered.

His eyes sliced into mine, searing me from the inside. "Hot. Because you're hotter than the blazing sun."

Kieran rolled his eyes. "Seriously, I think I'm going to be sick."

"He couldn't have said it better! See?" Julie exclaimed triumphantly. "We're meant to be together. I hate all that kissing, hugging, and all that gushy stuff people who are in *love* do. Unless it's ME!"

Laughing, I pulled away from Aidan and went about telling him each and every detail of my conversation with Julie, making sure not to omit anything. By the time I finished, Aidan and Kieran had devised the next step in our grand plan. They'd become members of the Night Guard. I didn't tell them that I harbored no intention to be kept out. Why should the guys have all the fun?

Chapter 10

After our conversation, Julie gave Kieran a peck on the cheek, said goodnight to me, and then disappeared into the night. I wondered if she decided to return to the morgue. Even though she couldn't see her body, she might still feel connected to it, but I didn't ask. For one, I didn't want to upset her, and then there was also the tiny possibility that she'd take it as an invitation to stay, which would've destroyed any prospect of spending some alone time with my boyfriend.

At the first light of dawn, Aidan and Kieran prepared to meet with the Council. It was a *brethren thing*, as he called it, meaning we had around twenty to thirty men gathered in our living room and they were talking about battles, allegiances, and yet more battles with lots of blood. I tried to blend in with the furniture as I stifled a yawn, bored out of my mind.

Logan—dressed in dark clothes with what looked like leather armor adorning his broad chest—shot me a wide smile and I inched closer to exchange a few words with me.

"You're beauty personified. It's only fitting that you share a bond with our leader," Logan said, planting a soft kiss on my hand, sending my cheeks on fire. The guy sure knew how to flatter a woman.

"Thank you."

His dark eyes glittered for a moment. "I hope I'll meet my bonded mate one day and that she'll be as good to me as you are to Aidan."

"You will," I whispered, smiling. "So, how old are you? Please excuse my curiosity, but I don't know much about you or warlocks in general."

He laughed. "Older than you think. See, we're not immortal like vampires, but the magic in our veins keeps us young and healthy for a long time. We live much longer than mortals...unless we're killed."

"Interesting," I said, sensing Logan was the right guy to get lots of information from. Aidan signaled the others to prepare for leaving, so I moved on to the next question burning on my tongue. "What is this brethren thing?"

Logan looked at Aidan, as though to get his approval. When he nodded, Logan turned back to me. "We're warriors who had the privilege to fight alongside Aidan. You could say that he saved our lives at one point or another, meaning our loyalty is bound to him by blood."

I had a bit of trouble to wrap my head around the fighting part. Of course I knew Aidan had a past *before* I came along, but hearing it from someone who seemed to know him for ages, I couldn't help but feel I didn't know Aidan as well as I always thought I did.

"Basically, what you're saying is that you're ready to stand by him in the upcoming war," I said.

He inclined his head and grimaced. "Not quite. You see, our loyalty is also bound to Morganefaire through the oath we made when joining the Night Guard, which makes this situation hard on us. We'll do our best to persuade the Council Aidan's the right person to support, but if the decision is made against him, then we'll be forced to take sides." He inched closer to whisper in my ear, "I know I'll serve Aidan, but I can't speak for the others."

I nodded gravely. "The more reason to work on our persuasion skills then."

Logan smiled and bowed his head. "It's not just about getting permission to fight beside him, but to be able to use our warlock blood as a weapon. Ever since it was abused hundreds of years ago, the practice has been punished with death. We want it back."

"Heard anything interesting?" Aidan said, appearing behind me. I nodded and let him wrap his arms around me to draw me close, his lips capturing my mouth in a tender kiss.

"It's all way more complicated than I thought," I whispered.

"Hopefully not for much longer." He let go of me with a disappointed sigh. "We expect the Council to come to a decision soon. Want to join us?"

I shook my head. "Thanks but I think I'll be staying here." I didn't want to mention in front of Logan that I intended to spend more time with Julie in order to find out more about the Night Guard.

Aidan's mouth locked on mine again and for a moment my mind turned blank from the tingling sensation his lips sent through my body. I rose on my toes to savor the sensation of his skin against mine.

"I'll try to be back soon," he whispered. I nodded and watched the procession leave.

***

The morning was still young, the green leaves covered in dew, as I made myself a cup of steaming coffee and ventured into the backyard in search of Julie. Even though I couldn't drink it, I loved the scent of it. Besides, the heat emitted by the hot liquid made my skin tingle and reminded me of the life I once led. I didn't want to lose that connection so I had made it a habit to brew a cup every morning and carry it around like I did when I was mortal.

I found Julie under a weeping willow with branches so low, they looked like hugging arms. She hovered a few inches above the ground. Around her, the black fog had spread like a macabre blanket that stood in contrast with her white complexion. The way her head bobbed to the left as she inspected a flower, lost in thought, made her look so alive I was almost fooled for a second. Then I remembered she was dead. She would never live again.

In terms of gossip Morganefaire couldn't be much different from other towns. Taking a deep breath, I scanned the area to make sure no one was watching us and it wouldn't look like I was talking into thin air, then inched closer, my feet pounding the grass to announce my presence. Julie only raised her head when I was a step or two away.

"Hey," she said flatly.

"I thought I might find you here." My eyes avoided her prodding gaze as I lowered myself onto the damp lawn and began picking at the dark green leaves of the weeping willow.

"This is my favorite tree in the world because it's so sad," Julie said. "It suits the mood in Morganefaire very well." Her expression changed from melancholy to despair. She was slowly beginning to understand the finiteness of her situation. I wanted to change the subject but she spoke first. "Once I realized I'd never know who my real family was, I wanted to get away from here as fast as I could and never look back. Take a trip around the world, maybe even find the perfect spot where I might just stay for a while, you know, grow roots." She shrugged and smiled bitterly. "I hope the afterlife makes up for it because it sure sucks to be dead."

I returned her smile but kept quiet. How could I tell her that the Otherworld was nothing but a constant loop of reliving your life's mistakes over and over again, until you could finally move into the light where there would be...nothing. No people, no new experiences, nothing but floating in a sense of wellbeing and happiness. Cass said that's what all souls looked forward to, but I doubted Julie, with her hunger for life and experiences, would be happy to hear that. I remained silent as I waited for her to resume the conversation.

"Last night when you were talking about what could've happened to me got me thinking." She turned to face me, her shimmering hazel eyes burning a hole in my heart. "You asked if I had any enemies, and as far as I know I don't have any because I never hurt anyone. But what if there was someone who hated me?"

I shook my head and reached out to grab her arm when I realized I'd most likely pass through her and upset her even more. So I drew back slowly. Sensing what I was about to do, she inched closer to me and placed her hand an inch away from mine. I stared at her porcelain skin and the soft, white glow it seemed to radiate.

"It was just a theory," I said looking up. "We're drawing at straws here."

She sighed. "But, as things stand, I think I'll trust your boyfriend's judgment. If he thinks something's wrong, then there probably is."

"Aidan's usually right," I said, my throat constricting at the sound of his name. Love washed over me and for a moment I saw his picture before my open eyes. So beautiful. So majestic. So near and yet so far away. Our bond made me ache for him whenever he wasn't around; made me miss his touch even though I knew I'd see him soon; made it hard to focus on anything but him.

"I've heard stories about him. He's dangerous," Julie said.

Aidan's picture dissipated. I frowned and turned back to her. "Really? What stories?"

"That he's a killer. That he can take one's heart out with a flick of his hand."

I smiled. "That's ridiculous."

"Is it?"

Her gaze met mine. For a moment I wasn't sure whether she was joking or dead serious, and then her lips curled into a smile. "They're just stories made up by superstitious idiots. Obviously, I don't believe a word. But the other one—"

"Kieran," I offered.

"Kieran." She rolled the name on her tongue. "He looks like he could kill with a single kiss. You should hook me up with him."

I laughed, until her grave expression told me she wasn't kidding this time. My laughter died in my throat. "He has a girlfriend," I muttered. It wasn't even a lie. He was sort of dating someone, or so Aidan said. I had yet to hear Kieran utter those words.

"So?" Julie shrugged. "I don't see a ring on his finger. Until I see a ring, he's game." I snorted. The girl couldn't be serious. She must've forgotten one thing: she was dead. Julie continued, not in the least bothered. "Besides, he didn't know me when he met her, so he couldn't compare us to see he and I would've been a match made in heaven. I think if he did, he would've chosen me."

I hurried to change the subject. "So you wanted to join the Night Guard, huh? Why?"

"Because it's the only way to get out of Morganefaire."

"Right." I nodded and tapped my fingers against my thigh, gathering my thoughts. I had no idea where to even begin this investigation. For all I knew, there could be a clue in everything Julie shared with me, or it could all be random, irrelevant small talk. Right now, I was ready to bet my non-existent wages on the latter. "We met one of the Night Guard guys in the Council hall when he carried—" your body, I wanted to say but didn't, "when he came to talk to us. His name was Iain. Do you know him?"

"I told you I know everybody," Julie said proudly. "Iain was the one to recruit me."

"Did any of your friends join?"

She shook her head. "He only asked me."

My curiosity piqued, I made a mental note to tell Aidan, then moved on to my next question. "So he knocked at the door and told you about the Night Guard recruiting for the Blue Moon?"

She shook her head again. "Nope. I was at Elyssa's, looking for some stuff, when I overheard her and Iain talking, so I asked whether they'd take on girls and he said they might. He said he'd put in a good word." I nodded encouragingly. She moistened her lips in thought and continued. "A few days later, we met there and he said he got me an interview."

"Who interviewed you?"

"One of the Council members, Logan," Julie said. "A few days later, I started my training. The night before—" she waved her hand expressively "—you know, I met Iain at Elyssa's and he told me I had passed."

"You keep mentioning Elyssa," I said. "Is she a friend?"

"She's the owner of Bells, Books & Candles. It's the dime store across the street from where I live. I can take you there if you want."

"Maybe." I looked at the sunless sky. The cool morning air had warmed up a bit, but it would be a while until the sun would peek from behind the rainclouds. I feared the sun as much as I feared being alone around mortals. At this point, I could no longer trust my vampire nature not to do what it wanted to do. I was thankful Julie was a ghost. If I lost control, the worst that could happen was that I might attack and glide right through her. She was completely safe around me. "Yeah, I think we should go."

"I loved hanging around that place for hours," Julie said with such enthusiasm it was contagious. "I bet you've never seen anything like it. We should go now!" Her eyes sparkled as she jumped up from her sitting position and reached out for me. I raised my hand to touch hers. The electric jolt was different from the one I felt whenever Aidan and I touched, but by no means unpleasant. She seemed to feel it too for she pulled back, then reached out again, laughing. "How did you do that?"

"I didn't. It must've been you."

She laughed her crystalline laughter again. "Yeah, probably. Must be a ghost thing." Her hand sliced right through me as she tried to grab my arm, sending another jolt through my body. If it upset her that she couldn't hold onto me, she didn't show it.

I followed her through the narrow streets, past cartwheels filled with fruit and vegetables, and market stands offering all kinds of merchandise, from garments to spices and used steel. Under a protective layer of clothes and with the sky clouded, the rays of sun didn't get to me as much as usual so I could enjoy the new world all around me. Julie talked non-stop, pointing at this and that. She didn't exaggerate when she claimed to know everyone. Throughout our little trip she not only recalled everyone's name but also their profession and their relation to her. By the time we reached the south side of the city and turned into a narrow street off the main road, I could only marvel at Julie's memory. I didn't even realize she stopped talking until I had almost crossed the street.

Frowning, I stopped and peered around me, wondering where Julie disappeared.

She lingered near a stall selling apples, hovering in mid-air as she pressed her nose against the fruit as though trying to smell it.

I ran back to her and greeted the owner—an old, sturdy woman with an infectious smile—then hissed, "What are you doing? Stop sniffing."

"She sells twenty-five varieties. Take your pick," Julie said.

"I wish I could." I missed eating food so badly. Especially apple pie. Dallas and I used to pick apples from our own apple tree when we were kids, before he grew up and turned into an irritating moron. We'd grab as many as we could and then head home and watch my mother make pies and what else not. It was one of my favorite memories.

"Well, taste one," Julie urged. "Go on. Do it!"

I shook my head. "No, I don't have much money on me." Telling her the truth that I was a vampire might have been a better idea, but somehow she seemed to believe I was just a mortal necromancer and I didn't want to upset her. Or maybe I enjoyed seeming normal for a change. Either way, I couldn't tell her—not yet.

"If you don't take an apple, I'm going to—" Julie pushed out her lower lip like a spoiled child. I planted my hands on my hips as I regarded her.

"Stop pushing me. I told you I don't have any coins on me and besides, I just got fired from my housekeeping job."

"You poor dear," the old woman said, inching closer. She must've overheard my conversation with Julie, thinking I was talking to her—or maybe to myself. "Take an apple. You're new in town and down on your luck, but don't worry, things will get better soon." She pressed a large apple into my hand, then turned her back on me and went about her business.

My cheeks flushed. I didn't want to be rude and say no, but she thought I was a beggar. I couldn't let her think that. "Sorry, I think you got it all wrong."

"Now try it," Julie yelled in my ear, making me jump a step back.

"Go away," I said through gritted teeth. The old woman shot me a sideway glance, as though I was deranged or something. Julie turned away, knocking down one apple. It was like a domino effect. I stared in horror as a bunch of them rolled down by my feet and onto the cobblestone path. My hand flew up to catch them, but I couldn't catch them all. The old woman's mouth pressed into a thin line, probably thinking I was the biggest troublemaker she'd ever met. But I had never been one a day in my life. Well, not deliberately. Needless to say, I was mortified.

"I'm so, so sorry." I muttered, trying to grab as many apples as I could hold. "I don't know how it happened." Oh, I knew how. It was all Julie's fault!

"Please, dear, just leave them," the old woman said with a pained expression. Even though it wasn't really my fault, I felt awfully guilty.

To my chagrin, Julie laughed and wiped a tear from her eyes. Clearly, she found the whole situation very amusing. I couldn't say the same thing about me. Julie had found a way to entertain herself, and that's a dangerous thing for a ghost. From the corner of my eye, I noticed the diabolic smile spreading across her lips as she began to tip over the cart, left and right, as though it was a cradle. My fingers shot up to steady it as I began to rearrange the apples—or as many as I could gather from the street.

"Julie, stop it or I'm leaving." I hissed as quietly as I could, hoping she'd hear me.

"What's wrong with her?" a young woman to my right whispered.

"She's a foreigner," her companion replied, as though that might be the perfect explanation for my erratic behavior. More people started to point and stare, and I realized that talking to thin air was making me look like a nut case.

Julie laughed. My blood ran hot and cold. "You're a lunatic!" I hissed at her. "I can't get rid of you. You just follow me around and annoy me. Did anyone ever tell you that you're a little bossy?"

The old woman's eyes reflected her anger, and who could blame her? Julie was destroying her livelihood, and I was taking the blame for it. "Please, be on your way," the woman said to me, eyes narrowed, nostrils flaring. Apologizing a few times, I fished several coins Aidan gave me out of my purse and paid her for her troubles, then disappeared around the corner. When I stopped my cheeks were on fire.

"I could kill you for making the poor woman's life hell," I said to the irritating ghost.

Her laughter instantly died in her throat and her expression turned serious. I bit my lip, realizing I had put my foot in my mouth and said the wrong thing yet again. Did she really think I wanted to kill her? I was mad but not *that* mad.

"I'm sorry, Julie, I didn't mean it. It's just a saying, you know." I bit my lip hard.

She frowned. "You know, I wasn't like this until now. I did everything they wanted me to do. I followed all the rules. I tried to live up to everyone's expectations. I was everyone's friend, which is why I don't understand why it happened to me. I'm fuming mad, mostly because I should've lived when I had the chance. And now it's too late." In some way I could understand her. "Why didn't you just take a bite? That's all I wanted," Julie continued.

I regarded the innocent expression on her angelic face, the exact opposite from the demonic smile she had sported only a minute or two ago. Maybe she wasn't the brightest star or maybe it was her character to ignore everything around her. Either way, I couldn't be angry with her. "You've been around me for more than a day now. Have you seen me eat or drink, or do anything mortals do?" Her jaw dropped. "I'm sorry, I didn't mean to be so rude before," I said. "I think the sun's getting to me."

"Why didn't you just tell me you were a vampire?" Julie whispered.

I shrugged and moistened my lips, considering my words. "You would've been scared, and I didn't want to add to your problems and worries."

She smiled and reached out her hand to touch my shoulder. A familiar electric jolt ran through me where her ghostly fingers brushed the thick material of my shirt. "You're not scary. A bit annoying, maybe, but definitely someone I like to have around. And I'm not saying that because I'm dead and have no friends."

"Likewise." The word made it past my lips before it dawned on me what I was saying, but I realized it was the truth. Even though Julie was irritating the hell out of me, I liked having her around.

"Look, we're here," Julie said, pointing at a gray building that blended in with the ones to its left and right. "That's where I live. And that's the dime store." I followed her line of vision to the other side of the road, and for a brief second I was sent back in time to a different place.

"It looks just like—"

"A tiny fairytale castle, right?" Julie exclaimed.

I crossed the street and stopped in front of the white walls and the wooden plate inscribed with the words BELLS, BOOKS & CANDLES in fancy cursive. Even without the snow to build the backdrop, the shop had an uncanny resemblance to a bakery in the Swiss Alps.

With a glance over my shoulder, I tried to push the door open a few times. It didn't budge until a voice called from inside, "Come in."

Chapter 11

The door opened slowly, as though invisible hands moved it, leaving an uneasy feeling in my stomach. I stepped in and scanned the deserted shop floor. The first thing I noticed upon entering BELLS, BOOKS & CANDLES was the sheer amount of décor, and by that I mean lots of what every normal human being would call clutter. There were statues of all sizes, shaped in any possible form, from animals to various mythological deities to hearts and stars, and miniature replicas of famous sights like the *Eifel Tower* and the *Statue of Liberty*.

I ran my finger across an ivory bowl and the matching grinder, marveling at how smooth the stone seemed, when I felt someone's presence behind me. My head turned sharply, my senses heightened to detect any approaching danger.

"Namaste. I'm Elyssa. Welcome to Bells, Books and Candles. How can I help you?" the woman said, taking a tiny bow. She was a few years older than me, with dark brown, cascading hair brushing her chin and shoulders. A warm smile spread across her pale face with high cheekbones and chocolate brown eyes that seemed to have a greenish shimmer to them. A chiffon, rainbow-colored dress hugged her body like a sheath.

I returned the smile but remained guarded. "I'm just browsing. Your shop looks very interesting from outside."

"You're not from here." Her voice was friendly and pleasant, but there was a hint of frostiness in it that I didn't notice before, as though she didn't like non-residents of Morganefaire very much. Or maybe it was just one of Aidan's companions she didn't want around.

I laughed softly. "What gave me away?"

She shook her head and narrowed her eyes. "The fact that you're not aware of Morganefaire's customs. You're in need but instead of asking for what you want, you pretend nothing's wrong."

"What makes you say that?" I wore nice clothes. My shoes didn't have holes in them. My boyfriend was loaded and one of the most powerful vampires out there. I tried to make sense of her words.

"I can *feel* you're in dire straits. We're not afraid to admit when we need something desperately," Elyssa said.

The woman was spot on, but I wasn't going to admit anything to a stranger because it could make us appear weak. Messing up Aidan's chances of gaining the city's support was no option. The magic would give us the advantage we needed in the upcoming war.

Elyssa wrapped her pale fingers around what looked like a golden flask and held it up, jolting me out of my thoughts. The soft sunshine caught in the dark green glass and made the liquid inside shimmer almost black.

"What's that?" I asked. She was drawing me in and I couldn't help but be mesmerized.

"A magic potion that holds the power of the universe," Elyssa said. "It's one of the many things we have on offer."

"Have you used it before?"

Elyssa nodded. "Many times. I've cured the sick, and mended broken hearts. I've brought happiness upon those who sought it, and destroyed others' enemies. But those are all wishes that need to be spoken out before they can manifest."

My heart hammered hard as something dawned on me. The Shadow magic infused into Kieran's blood during the ritual was passed onto me when I was turned, and it had worked...until something broke it, triggering my bloodlust and the sensitivity to light. Morganefaire was a strong source of magic. Even if this woman offered only bogus potions and strangely shaped semi-precious gemstones, the real magic had to be somewhere. If I found it, then I might just get rid of the bloodlust. I had no idea where it could be but I could multi-task...solve Julie's murder and my sunburn dilemma.

"Let me know if you have any questions and I'll be happy to assist you," Elyssa said. With a last smile she stepped quickly behind a transparent curtain, then disappeared.

"Wait!" I trailed after her and pulled the curtain aside. Behind it was nothing but a white wall. Where had she gone? "Julie," I whispered, frowning. "Julie, where are you?"

"Over here," she said.

I followed her voice around a few cabinets filled to the brim with yet more clutter. She was hovering near a stand with paintings in silver frames. I inched closer and trailed her line of vision to an image depicting a tall wall rising against the black night. Countless arms and hands, buried beneath the ground, seemed to erupt out of the earth and reach for the wall, their pale skin catching the soft glow of the moon and stars above. It was a creepy image that sent shivers down my spine.

"What's that?" I whispered.

"The wall that keeps the darkness out," Julie said. "The Night Guard patrols it to make sure nothing enters the gate or climbs inside the city."

I thought back to Aidan's words. After centuries of being hunted by mortals, the witches and warlocks of Morganefaire had become distrustful of the outside world, and who could blame them? Had I seen friends or family being burned alive during witch-hunts, or tortured into admitting the most sordid accusations, I might've started to dislike the world outside of my city as well.

"Being chosen to serve the Night Guard is an honor," Julie said with a sigh.

"Is that why you disappeared last night? To watch the wall?" The question made it past my lips before I could contain myself, but she didn't seem to mind my prying.

"Yeah." She turned to face me, her expression grave. "It was very quiet." A flicker appeared in her eyes, and I knew she kept something to herself.

"What did you see?"

She shook her head. "I'm just a ghost so I don't see. I sense. But it's nothing."

"What was it, Julie?"

She grimaced. "I don't know. The night was darker than ever before, that's all." She laughed softly. "You'll think me nuts."

"No, I won't. You need to tell me because it might be important."

"Okay." She took a deep breath, gathering her words. "I was marching up and down the wall when one of the torches illuminating the street below went out. Everything was black. It was really creepy."

"Maybe someone blew out the fire," I suggested.

She shook her head again. "I don't think so. Have you ever seen one of the night torches lining the streets? It's a huge thing. The flames don't even flicker. You'd need a lot of breath to blow that fire out."

"It could've been the wind."

"Maybe," Julie said flatly, "except that—" She hesitated, then nodded. "No, you're right. It must've been the wind."

Her expression told me she wasn't convinced but I didn't insist. She had been scared so, naturally, she paid importance to something that was just a coincidence. What bothered me more were Elyssa's words. Part of me wanted to ask Julie if Elyssa's magic was real. Could she help me? Or was she just a gypsy selling a bunch of nonsense to make a quick buck? The other part of me couldn't tell Julie about my problems. I didn't want her to pity me the way Aidan and Kieran did. Things were complicated enough.

"I'd like to talk to Elyssa, maybe ask her a few questions," I said, changing the subject. "Do you know where I can find her?"

"Probably in her office down the hall." Julie pointed to a narrow door obscured by a curtain I didn't notice before. "She likes to give her customers privacy."

That surprised me. "Where I come from people would rob her blind."

"No one would ever dare steal anything from her," Julie said.

"Why's that?"

Julie shrugged and turned away, as though she had already lost interest in our conversation, which didn't surprise me. In addition to unpredictable mood swings, ghosts also had a notoriously short attention span.

Leaving Julie to her thoughts, I stepped through the curtain hesitantly and found myself in a narrow hallway with white walls. On the other end were several closed doors. I tried the first—a closet with merchandise and price tags. The one opposite from it led into another hall with a staircase. I was about to shrug it off as a back entrance and close the door again when my heightened senses picked up a strange noise.

I stopped in my tracks and held my breath to listen. For a few seconds nothing stirred, and then there it was again: a sharp breath followed by a tiny whimper, as though someone inhaled and the action pained them. Frowning, I took a step forward when I felt someone's presence behind me.

"Can I help you with anything?" Elyssa asked.

I turned sharply, my eyes growing wide the way they always did when guilt flooded trough me. "I was looking for you and didn't know which way to go."

She waited until I stepped back into the hall and then she closed the door behind me, making sure to lock it up.

"Let's go back to the shop," she said. I nodded and followed her, then took the seat she offered me near the window overlooking the busy street.

"Would you like some tea?" she asked. I smelled the delicious aroma of peaches. For a second I wondered if I should have a cup but, knowing it wouldn't do my stomach any favors, I shook my head in response. She smiled and continued, "I'll have some if you don't mind." I watched her as she poured herself a cup from a china pot on a nearby side table, and then joined me at the table. Her chiffon dress with its rainbow colors reflected the light as she arranged it around her delicate body.

"When did you stop drinking anything but blood?" she started.

The question took me by surprise. I had no idea whether to disclose the truth or pretend I didn't hear her and change the subject. In the end I decided I had nothing to hide. By now everyone in Morganefaire must've heard the visitors were vampires so it wasn't a big deal. "A few weeks ago," I said. "I've been missing it terribly. How did you know?"

"You couldn't open the door to the shop. That usually means one thing—you're a supernatural," she said. "Either Shadow, lykae, or vampire. Definitely not deity or demon, and since Shadows and lykae haven't crossed Morganefaire's walls in centuries, you could only be a vampire. Though I have to admit the daylight walking threw me off for a second." Her intense gaze focused on me, making me feel as though she could peer right into my soul. "Did you come here to ask for your old life back? Because Morganefaire has the power to grant it if that's what you want."

My heart almost stopped as all my moments with Aidan perished and my old life flashed before my eyes: returning to my matchbox room in London, dating some guy I didn't really love, working part-time while trying to save money for an undergraduate degree. Living a normal life—for a while I thought I wanted it back. That time was over.

"No—" I shook my head vehemently "—that part of me is dead now. I have a new life with my boyfriend whom I love with all my heart. Going back isn't an option."

"You're happy, I can see that in your eyes, but something's missing."

"Yes." I paused, hesitating.

Elyssa smiled and brushed a hand through her long honey locks, then peered around her, as though looking for something. "What you *want* is in here, but not what you need to do." She stood up and paced over to a cabinet, unlocked it with a key dangling from a chain, and pulled out a glass vial with beautiful silver ornaments and a dark red liquid.

"What's that?" I asked, craning my neck to get a better look.

Elyssa sat back down and held out her open palm. The vial shimmered. I didn't know whether she wanted me to touch it, or not. So I didn't, but my gaze remained glued to the tiny flask as something stirred within me. I didn't need her to tell me what was inside. My vampire nature could sense it without smelling or touching it.

Blood. And not just any but that of a Morganefaire witch.

"The blood contained in this amulet could be the answer to all of your problems. It's the last one ever created before the Council banned its sale. The magic inside keeps it from drying out," she whispered. "You have no idea how much it's worth."

Even though the blood must've been centuries old and probably way past its sell-by date to the extent of giving one blood poisoning, my mouth watered at the sight of it. I swallowed past the lump in my throat and ignored the raging hunger inside me.

"Aren't you scared it might fall into the wrong hands?" I asked.

She regarded me the way you'd regard a child that has yet to learn to understand connections. I instantly felt stupid for having asked such a question. "A wall of magic surrounds this shop. Nobody, not even a Shadow or a vampire, could ever break into my fortress."

"Could it help me?" I whispered.

Elyssa smiled self-assured. "Morganefaire's magic has never failed anyone."

My pulse raced a million miles an hour. I had no guarantee this woman was telling the truth. For all I knew she could be a delusional lunatic. And yet...for some reason I *needed* to believe because Kieran and Aidan were the living proof that magic worked. It could be a coincidence, but Elyssa's hints were undeniable. She knew what others didn't see. If she sensed what I needed, she might also have the solution to my cravings. I felt a rush of joy and hope that soon part of my troubles would be over. At least I could give it a try.

"I'll take it," I said maybe a tad too enthusiastically. "How much?"

She moistened her lips, hesitating. "I'm sorry, the vial's not for sale."

"Then why did you show it to me?" A wave of anger and disappointment washed over me.

"As I told you, want you want is in here but you need to present your case before the Council and get their approval first, and then we shall see." She hesitated before adding, "They might decide to make an exception."

Blurt out my secret? No way, and particularly not since she made it sound like I stood no chance anyway. I snorted and waved my hand expressively. "Forget it. It was a crazy idea."

She grimaced. "Well, in that case—" Her voice trailed off. A moment of silence ensued between us.

Remembering what I actually came for, I resumed the conversation. "A girl you know, Juliette Baron—Julie, died recently. I'd like to ask you a few questions about her."

Elyssa looked up, confused, and a shadow crossed her face. "You know Juliette?"

"She's a friend." Or should I have said an annoying ghost that followed me day and night until I solved her death?

Elyssa's eyes narrowed slightly. "I wasn't aware she knew people outside of Morganefaire."

"It was a pen pal thing," I said. Elyssa's unconvinced expression told me she didn't believe a word.

"Tell her that I told you all about how she set her mentor's shop on fire the first time she tried her hand at magic," Julie whispered in my ear. I relayed her words to Elyssa, whose expression didn't change.

"It's a well-known story anyone could've told you," Elyssa said.

"What no one knows is that you were once engaged to be married with someone living outside of Morganefaire." Watching Elyssa intently, I repeated Julie's words. "You gave him up because you feared the Council might find out and something might happen to you."

I tried not to smile as she turned a shade paler. She clasped her hands in her lap so hard her knuckles shimmered white. "You're here for Julie's funeral, then?" Her voice was smooth and composed, but there was a sharp edge to it.

"Yes." I nodded to emphasize the word.

Her expression darkened. "It's unfortunate that she's no longer with us, but she had always been of poor health so it didn't come as a surprise to any of us."

"She's lying," Julie whispered behind me. Fighting the urge to turn around and converse wit her, I pressed my open palms against the smooth table, ready to start digging.

"I never knew she was in poor health? How so?" I asked.

"Well—" Elyssa took a deep breath and moistened her lips as she considered her words "—she used to be sick a lot, always complaining about this and that. She wasn't as agile or gifted as the others."

I didn't need Julie's hiss in my ear that it was another blatant lie to know Elyssa wasn't telling the truth. She was scared—I could read that much from the way her gaze darted across the table.

"She loved this shop and used to spend a lot of time in here," I said.

"How do you know?" Elyssa asked sharply. Her eyes reflected her mistrust.

I pointed around me. "It's a beautiful place. What girl wouldn't?"

Her stance relaxed a little. "Julie used to sit in the corner over there." She raised her chin to the right. "It was her favorite spot for reading."

"What was she interested in?"

"I'm not sure. Travelling, I think."

"Did she ever tell you she wanted to leave Morganefaire?" I asked.

Elyssa's soft laughter rang through the air. I marveled at how fake it sounded. "Why would she ever want to leave?"

I raised my brows. "Did she ever mention it?"

My question silenced her for an instant. Her eyes scanned the floor, then the displays to her right. Either she was thinking back to her conversations with Julie, or she was preparing to lie and needed to prepare her words.

"I don't think she did," Elyssa said eventually. "I didn't know her well."

"That's not true," Julie whispered. "I mentioned it a few times. She laughed it off."

I nodded to let Julie know I had acknowledged her words. "What about the Night Guard? Did she ever mention she wanted to join it?"

"Who are you and what's your business?" Her eyes narrowed to two tiny slits. I was taken aback, partly because I didn't expect this hostility and partly because I thought she'd be happy to talk about Julie. Somehow I had the impression the two of them had been close, that they had shared secrets with one another. That she pretended otherwise didn't make any sense.

"Did I fail to introduce myself?" I reached out my hand. She ignored it, so I pulled back. "So sorry. My name's Amber Reed. I'm here for Julie's funeral. I hope my questions don't bother you, but her death has come unexpected. It's left me shocked and sleepless, so I'd like to know more about my dear friend."

Her expression remained blank, as though she had no idea who I was. For once, I believed her.

"She wanted to join the Night Guard," Elyssa said. "The poor girl didn't live to see her life-long dream accomplished." For a woman who claimed not to know Julie particularly well, it was a strange statement. And then she did something that instantly raised my suspicion. She stood and smiled the way people smile when they want you gone. Her lips curved into an ugly, exaggerated smirk. Her eyes shined but the fragile skin around them didn't crease. Her friendliness wasn't genuine; it was a ploy to brush me off without causing mistrust.

"Thank you for stopping by," she said. "If I remember anything else, I'll make sure to contact you, Amber."

I nodded. "I'd appreciate it so much. And I know Julie would too."

Julie rolled her eyes at me.

"Let me assist you to the door," Elyssa said.

I didn't budge from the spot. "This place is fascinating. If you don't mind I'd like to browse around some more."

She hesitated briefly, obviously not keen on the idea of me lingering here. And then another fake smile brightened her features, and I wondered how I could've been so stupid to fall for it when I first saw her. "I'll be more than happy to assist you up front. Pick the item you like and I'll meet you at the register."

Gosh, she wanted me gone big time. I had never felt so unwelcome in my life. Turning my back on her, I marched over to the spot she had pointed out before. So, Julie had been sitting here for hours, lost in books. I slumped onto a chaise longue and put my feet up as I tried to step into another world. The world of a girl who never got to meet her parents; who had the life-long wish to get away from here in the hope to mark her place in the world outside those walls.

"I remember sitting here only a few days ago, flicking through a book with the most beautiful beaches in the world," Julie said flatly. My gaze fell on the shiny cover of a coffee table book depicting a beautiful white beach under an impossibly blue sky. As I looked up, I noticed the shelf display carved into the wall. I came to my feet slowly, my eyes narrowing on the cabinet. On the top shelf was a shiny object that shimmered in soft, dark-green hues.

Interested, I inched closer to inspect a ring sitting on a black cushion. The emerald stone was set in an intricate gold setting adorned with tiny symbols. My breath caught in my throat. It looked just like the ring I once saw dangling from Aidan's chain and on Rebecca's finger after she had taken it with her to her grave. The gold was infused with witch's blood and could trace any person or object, dead or alive, which is how Rebecca tracked me down in Hell at Cass's birthday party. Aidan told me three rings were created but he didn't know where the third was. Could I have just located the missing one? This place needed security big time, and yet I couldn't see a burglar alarm or shatterproof glass. I couldn't even sense an energy field that might indicate the ring was protected by magic. It was strange.

"Have you found anything you'd like?" Elyssa asked from behind me.

I pointed at the ring. "That one."

"It's beautiful, isn't it? The detail is exquisite." She opened the glass door and retrieved the black box. "Would you like it gift-wrapped?"

I nodded. "Yeah, that'd be great."

"I bet it's something you've never seen before," she said, suddenly eager to make small talk.

"Oh, I have." I smiled mischievously as I thought back to the morning when Aidan first showed me the ring and told me its story.

"Really?" Elyssa's brows shot up.

"My boyfriend has one of those," I said. Aidan would be so surprised to know I found another that looked just like it.

"How lovely." Elyssa walked over to her counter and wrapped the box in red tissue paper, then handed it to me. I retrieved my wallet to pay but she shrugged it off. "It's a gift," she said.

"Thank you but I couldn't possibly accept it."

"But I insist. Think of it as a token of my appreciation for looking into my dear Julie's death." Gazing into my eyes, she pushed the tiny package into my hand. "Namaste, Amber Reed. I hope we'll meet again."

Chapter 12

Elyssa had not behaved the way I expected but I attributed her cagey and secretive attitude to not wanting to raise suspicion. And who could blame her? A girl she knew was dead, a girl who had frequented her shop. It was a natural reaction to keep one's mouth shut so I didn't dwell on it. BELLS, BOOKS & CANDLES had been a dead end, but not a complete waste of time. Hurrying my step, I almost bounced through the narrow streets, barely noticing the vendors' colorful booths and stands that had fascinated me only an hour ago. I might not have gotten rid of my bloodlust, but I had discovered a way that might just work, which I had to share with Aidan. Right after I gave him the package in my hand. I couldn't wait to see his expression.

The way home seemed to take forever, not least because Julie just wouldn't shut up. Nodding every now and then, I tuned out and focused on my own thoughts...until a strong jolt jerked me out of my reverie.

"What?" I muttered, rubbing my arms. I hated it when ghosts got physical to get my attention.

"You're not listening!" Julie yelled in my ear. "I've been thinking."

I took a step to my right to put some distance between us, and sighed, sensing I was forced to listen now.

"I think we should forget about all of this murder stuff for a little while," Julie continued. "Let's do what I've been dying to do for years."

"Okay, I'll bite. What's that?"

"Let's leave this city and let the wind take us where it will." Like on cue, a soft breeze wafted past, ruffling her hair. I shook my head, wondering how she did that.

"We're not leaving," I said and hurried my pace. Even if I tried, I couldn't outrun her, but pretending felt good enough.

"Fine, then let's talk about Kieran because I think he was totally checking me out."

"He can't see you, Julie."

She shrugged. "He can sense how hot I am."

I felt like I was sixteen again. "He probably can," I said to appease her.

Thick clouds darkened the sky above, then cleared again. The air smelled damper than before. In a few hours, rain would pour down on Morganefaire. I loved to feel the charged particles on my skin.

We walked in silence for all of a minute, Julie lost in her thoughts, me enjoying the feeling of oncoming rain. And then she started again. "You know, I've got a million questions. Could garlic keep you and your clan from devouring my friends?"

"I have no plans to devour your friends," I said slowly, irritation creeping up on me.

She tapped a finger against her lips. "How did you become a vampire?" I opened my mouth to answer when her face lit up and she floated up and down, making me think she had come up with something meaningful to ask. "How about a large black cape? Do you wear one?" She tilted her head. "It's kind of out of style now with vampires. Even though your wardrobe needs a little shape and color, you seem quite modern and you definitely talk like my generation."

I groaned inwardly. "Seriously, that's your important question? Asking me whether I'm wearing a cape? Why don't you just ask me if I sparkle while you're at it?"

"Sparkle? Since when do vampires sparkle?"

I waved my hand. "It's a *Twilight* thing."

She shrugged and then continued, "So do you think if I'm stuck in this world you could set me up with a hot ghost?"

"I don't know." My shoulders slumped. Why wouldn't she just shut up? I was ready to start begging.

"You should be able to do that because you're a necromancer and all," Julie said, completely unaware of the effect she had on me. "Can you call a ghost any time you want?"

"I'm new to all of this," I muttered. "Besides, I really doubt this gift was given to me so I can hook up people."

"You mean you weren't born with it?" She sounded genuinely surprised. "I don't get it. How does the whole summoning thing work? Do you need candles? Do you want me to chant? Because I'm really good at it."

"Julie—" I stopped in mid-stride, ready to talk some sense into her. Several people turned to watch the loony woman talking into thin air, but I didn't care. It was a matter of keeping my sanity intact. "Look, I'm still trying to deal with it. It's not been easy. So, please, can we talk about it another time? It's a touchy subject for me."

"Fine," Julie said smiling. For a whole second I thought she sympathized with me...until her grin turned into a grimace and she opened her mouth again. "I've never met a necromancer afraid of ghosts. Although, I never met a necromancer before at all. How does one get that title and become a vampire at the same time? That's so cool. I'd love to be a vampire. But I'm not sure about the whole sleeping in a coffin thing. Wait!" She slapped my arm, sending an electric jolt through it. I could almost see the metaphorical light bulb going on over her head. "How come you're not sleeping in a coffin?" Her brows shot up. "Or are you? A coffin must be difficult to hide...unless it's in the basement or the morgue. Is that why you ventured down there?"

"Julie, please." I sighed exasperated. "Just shut up."

"Fine, you don't want to talk about it," she said, taking off through the busy streets. I hurried after her, lest I lose her in the crowd and have to teleport home. Come to think of it, maybe teleporting with its nausea and weakening effect on me wasn't such a bad idea compared to Julie's rambling. "Let me tell you this funny story," she continued. "There was this guy who sold animal manure and he had this hot son. I mean, flowing blond hair and smoldering dark eyes." She started to fan herself. "I was hoping he'd ask me out to the Moonlight Dance at the harvest festival. So I was like..."

My hands clenched into fists. Counting the seconds, I bit my lower lip until the thin, protective layer burst. Drawing my own blood was a dangerous thing that could turn me into a rampant killer, but I had to do something that would help me tune out the irritating ghost.

Chapter 13

When we finally reached the front door, I breathed out relieved. Probably tired of her own chatter, Julie told me she wanted to sit on the porch...and think, God bless her. I breezed into the living room, expecting Aidan and Kieran to be sitting on the sofa, waiting for me. To my disappointment, I found Maya dusting the shiny cherry wood table. A plastic cleaning box with a bare minimum of cleaning supplies—an unlabeled bottle of clear fluid, paper towels and a rag— was sitting at her feet. She didn't raise her gaze as I walked in.

A swirl of gritty dirt fell off my shoes as I neared the sofa. Maya rolled her eyes and reached for a broom and dustpan.

"I'm so sorry. I'll clean this up." I hurried to help her but she shooed me away.

"Don't be ridiculous. You're our guest," she said, finishing up. "Can I get you anything?"

She said all the right words but her tone sounded annoyed. I could see right past that fake act of hers. That eye roll said it all. "I'm fine, thanks." I set my purse down and looked around.

"They're not back yet," she said. I could see that much so I nodded.

She pressed her mouth into a thin line. The silence between us became downright embarrassing. I hovered in the doorway, unsure whether it'd be rude to excuse myself and head upstairs. In the end I decided my mother had taught me better than that. So what if she was a bit shy? Maybe she had yet to warm up to me. In the last few weeks, I had met my share of crazies. If she turned out to be a bit crazy, one more was no big deal.

"Do you live nearby?" I asked, slumping onto the sofa.

Maya mumbled something that sounded like 'yes' and began to rearrange the cushions on the sofa, keeping a good distance between us as she worked her way around me. I wondered whether I looked like I had the plague or something. Ignoring her downright derisive attitude, I put on my brightest smile and continued, "Today I visited the market. It's such a beautiful place."

This time she didn't even bother to answer. I fought back a frown and kept my smile in place even though my mouth was slowly beginning to hurt from the effort. But I wasn't ready to give up yet. "We've never thanked you for taking such good care of us. So, thank you."

She nodded, then started to polish the already sparkling glass cabinet. Her back was turned on me, but I could see her face in the reflection of the glass. The woman was about as social as my cupboard. I heaved a silent sigh and drummed my fingers on my thigh.

"I bought my boyfriend an awesome present," I said.

Maya ignored me. I couldn't tell whether it was just an act or whether she didn't hear a word I said. Either way, I was bored enough to want to find out. I shuffled in my seat to get a better glimpse at her face. "On the way home, I was chased by giant demon dogs. And now you ask me...how did I survive? I pulled out my magic sword, jumped on their back and slayed them."

No answer. Her expression remained the same. No twitching lips, no irritated eye roll. Heck, not even a shift in gaze. How could anyone switch off like that? Maya was creepier than I thought. She reminded me of a robot on automatic, continuing to polish the glass cabinet, which was already as shiny as new.

Okay, she didn't want to talk. I decided to give up and turned my attention to my nails. I always did that when I was nervous: inspecting them, cleaning them, biting them. Something stirred in my line of vision. I looked up at the glass cabinet and noticed Maya staring at my reflection. Her dark eyes shimmered unnaturally bright. When she noticed me looking she averted her gaze, but not fast enough. In that brief second I could swear a shadow crossed her features and her eye color turned from brown to a dark shade of green.

The whole situation reminded me of what I went through only a few days ago around the time my bloodlust flared up. My heart beat so hard I almost shook in my seat. It couldn't be happening again. Not after I just experienced a full-blown confrontation with a poltergeist and almost died at the hands of her werewolf pet. I couldn't go through it again. Jumping up, I excused myself and dashed out the door, and only stopped when I reached the backyard. "Get a grip," I mumbled, my feet pounding the grass. "You're being paranoid."

I took slow and deep breaths to steady myself. Only a few days ago, when I was possessed, my eye color had changed, which scared the crap out of everyone who knew me. But Maya showed no signs of being possessed. No screaming in horror and jumping out the window...like me. No rambling something about seeing blood pouring down the walls...like me again. Basically, I was a crazy whack job. It came as a surprise Aidan didn't throw a straitjacket on me. But Maya wasn't like that. The only thing that seemed strange about her was her unwillingness to communicate, but if an anti-social attitude is an indicator of ghostly possession, then half the world's population might be haunted.

I ran a hand through my hair as I sorted through my thoughts. Eventually, I decided there was nothing wrong with Maya. The eye color occurrence was nothing but a reflection of my own fears—and ever since entering Aidan's world I sure had accumulated a lot of those. My mind was basically playing a trick on me. Yeah, that had to be the answer. Unless Maya was some new supernatural creature I hadn't met yet.

I only realized it was already early afternoon when Aidan's voice echoed from the house a moment before he appeared around the corner.

"Hey," he said softly. The smile on his face disappeared quickly when he noticed my expression. Frowning, he gently grabbed my shoulders and forced me to look at him. "What's wrong?"

"Nothing, I—"

He arched a brow. I took a deep breath as I decided to be honest. No more secrets between us. "Okay, there was something. Maya was in the living room when I came back from my trip with Julie. She was strange, and then I thought I saw her eye color change, which made me wonder whether she's some supernatural creature I don't yet know about." The moment I finished, I realized how foolish I sounded. I almost expected Aidan to burst out in laughter and tell me I was behaving like a scared, little child, but he just continued to frown and remained silent.

"I'm pretty sure Maya's just a witch, like everyone else in Morganefaire," he finally said, hesitating, "but if she makes you feel uncomfortable I can get Blake to send a replacement."

"That's not what I meant. I told you it's nothing, so just forget about it." I took off toward the house. Aidan followed a step behind. I could feel his presence as though he was glued to me. "I wish someone could give me a giant handbook so I'm not constantly walking around in the dark," I muttered. He shot me an apologetic look. Before he could say a word, I held up my hand and continued. "Yeah, I know that doesn't exist."

He smiled. "But it should."

"Damn straight." I nodded. "I'm going to write one."

"Whatever you do I trust your instincts," he whispered. "Maya doesn't look dangerous, but you might be sensing her animosity toward strangers wafting from her. I don't want you to be upset because of it so it might be better to talk to Blake."

I turned to regard him. "No, let her stay. She might not like me very much, but that's not a reason to sack someone."

"Are you sure you want her around?" He wrapped his arms around me and pulled me closer. I nodded as I buried my head against his chest, breathing in his scent. A soft breeze ruffled our hair and caressed our skin, making me shiver.

"There's something I've been meaning to give you." My hand moved inside my back pocket to retrieve his present. I smiled as I watched him eye it carefully before tearing through the paper to reveal the black box beneath.

"What is it?" he asked.

I shrugged, amused. "Don't know. You tell me."

"Even though I've no idea what could possibly be inside, thank you." Aidan's words filled me with pride. My heart almost burst with love at the prospect of having removed one of his worries.

His fingers gingerly moved across the velvet cover and pried it open. The emerald stone shimmered in the daylight, catching my breath. A smile spread across my lips. I felt like jumping up and down, and hugging him at the same time. But when I raised my gaze to catch his expression, I realized he didn't share my enthusiasm.

"Thank you," he said again. "It's beautiful." His words were genuine but it wasn't the reaction I had expected.

I frowned, suddenly irritated with him. "It's the same ring you have. Don't you recognize it?"

"Babe—" a pause, then "—it's a replica."

"How can you tell? It looks exactly the same." I fought the urge to shake some sense into him because, the way I saw it, the ring couldn't possibly be a fake. Or could it?

His expression softened even more, as though he felt sorry for my blunder. Deep inside I cringed at my own naivety and stupidity. Of course the ring couldn't possibly be real. According to Aidan, it was one of the most sought-after objects in the paranormal world. So, why would it gather dust in a makeshift display in a witch's meaningless shop with no security to guard it? Because, obviously, it was indeed worthless. I felt my face drop the way Julie's had when I told her I couldn't try the apple because I was a vampire.

"It's a beautiful gift I'll treasure forever because it came from you," Aidan said. That about did it. I grabbed the box out of his hands and tossed it across the garden into the nearby bushes. A bird swooped over our heads and flew away, so I knew the darn ring landed somewhere. But where, I didn't care. I just wanted it gone forever.

"I'm such a moron," I muttered. "I can't believe I really thought I had solved that problem of yours after you spent hundreds of years trying to locate its whereabouts."

Laughing, Aidan took off through the bushes to search for the ring. I could only hope he wasn't going to tell his friends about his gift, or I might end up the laughing stock yet again. Slowly, I was getting used to my reputation— scaredy cat necromancer and newly turned vampire messes up big time...*again*.

"I forgot to tell you Kieran and I have joined the Night Guard," Aidan called from under the bushes. I rolled my eyes and slumped onto the lawn to pout for a minute. A bit later he joined me, holding the box in his hand and still laughing. "You wanna come?"

"You guys want me around?" I sat up instantly, the box in his hands forgotten or, better said, ignored. "No begging, no arguing?"

He shook his head and brushed a stray strand of hair out of my face. "No begging, no arguing. In fact, we hope you'll join us. You'll make a hell of a private investigator." His eyes sparkled and for a moment, I couldn't tell whether he meant it or was making fun of me. I decided it was probably the latter, but I didn't care. I had been dying to find out more about the Night Guard, and this was my chance.

"So the Council meeting went well?" I asked.

He cringed. "Not quite. There was a lot of talk about the coming war. Logan's on our side, but Riley wants to keep Morganefaire's allegiances open, meaning he thinks it might be wise to wait and see, and then kiss the winner—"

"Where the sun don't shine," I finished.

"I meant to say 'the winner's hand' but I guess your interpretation is spot on," Aidan muttered.

"That's bad."

He took a deep breath as his gaze swept over the blossoming rosebushes. "I talked to Blake." I reached out to brush my hand through his hair, signaling I was there for him, no matter what. "He agrees that Julie was murdered, but he has no idea why."

I nodded. "Thought that much."

"There's something else." His voice lowered to a mere whisper. "Another body was found this morning."

"What?" I inched closer, too shocked to form a coherent thought.

"She was only twenty and died in her sleep. Or so it seems. Blake's found out that she was about to start an apprenticeship outside of Morganefaire in a few days. The Council has decided to keep her death a secret, but it's only a matter of time until it leaks to the public." He closed his eyes and began to massage his temples the way he always did when he expected things to take a turn for the worse. "One death they might accept as a coincidence, two and they might think it could have something to do with us."

"A furious crowd demanding answers," I whispered. "Answers we don't have." He nodded. "Do you want me to visit her body and question her ghost?"

Aidan's lips pressed into a grim line. "It's probably too late. The reaper must've been here already."

"You don't know that for sure. Just look at Julie. There's no sign of a reaper and she's following me around like there's no tomorrow," I said, wondering why I hadn't seen her in a while. "It's worth a shot," I continued quieter in case anyone heard us. The idea of having a second ghost following me around scared the crap out of me, but I offered nonetheless in case it might do any good.

"I appreciate it," Aidan said. "But your hands are full with her, and one ghost is enough."

I tried not to show my relief. Julie was manageable...so far, but I definitely couldn't tune in to two ghosts at the same time. It'd drive me bonkers, not to mention the fact that they might just decide to possess me or something.

"Any clues as to what could've happened to them?" I asked.

"None. The Night Guard is our only chance." He inched closer until our lips almost touched. I could feel his hot breath on my skin and it sent shivers down my spine. "At this point we cannot trust anyone."

"Yeah, like they trust us." I snorted.

"Not true. They'll be wary of Kieran and me, because they think we have underlying motives. We're ancient vampires with a bad reputation. But you're a completely different story and could hide under the radar."

"Because I'm super sweet, friendly, and never have shed innocent blood." Well, except for one poor squirrel—may it rest in peace!

"My thoughts exactly. Everybody likes you—" he cringed "—except the help." I slapped his arm playfully. "But, seriously, you could mingle with the guards, play the loyal girlfriend supporting her man by being there, completely bored by the politics."

I wasn't even sure that wasn't the truth. "Got it. I'll pretend I'm bored out of my mind while I try to peer behind their armor, discover their secrets, and find the culprit."

He kissed me. "You're the smartest girl I know. I couldn't ask for a better equal. While I keep the guards busy you search for clues." He trailed his fingers down my neck as his blue gaze interlocked with mine. I stared at him, mesmerized. "Just don't stray too far and be careful. I couldn't bear if anything happened to you."

"When are we starting?" I managed to say, heart pounding and all.

"Tonight," he whispered. "When darkness descends you'll see the scariest thing of your life."

After my last possession and Rebecca's poltergeist activity, which almost made me want to lock myself up in a pretty, white cell, I highly doubted anything could scare me more. But I nodded nonetheless. As our lips connected in our first heated kiss of the day, it completely slipped my mind that I hadn't told him about my meeting with Elyssa.

"I wanted to give you a normal life, but at this point I doubt it's even possible," Aidan said, breaking away from me for a second.

"I'm in this relationship for the long haul and that's all that matters." Supernatural was my middle name now. I appreciated the fact that Aidan wanted to give me the perfect life with the white picket fence and all, but that was never going to happen. Not in his world. Not until we won the war.

"You're a cute addition to the paranormal community." His lips nuzzled my neck. I drew him closer and leaned back to enjoy his soft kisses, ready to forget the world around us. His hands trailed down my back and settled on my hips. I reached up his chest to loop my arms around his neck as his lips finally settled on mine in a long kiss. My legs wobbled beneath me, but Aidan held me tight as his lips brushed over mine in one eclectic kiss after another, making my head so dizzy I thought I might be standing in the center of a tornado.

Eventually he broke our embrace and walked over to what looked like a briefcase to retrieve a red plastic bag. "What's that?" My voice came low and hoarse as my head still floated in ecstasy.

"You need to drink...just in case," Aidan said. To my delight I realized his self-control didn't fare any better. His eyes burned with passion, though I couldn't tell whether for me or because of what was inside the bag.

I needed to feed. He was right about that. As much as I hated doing this, it'd buy me a few days of peace. I grabbed the bag from his outstretched hand and headed upstairs to lock myself inside the bathroom so no one would see me ravish my disgusting meal.

A few minutes later, I peeled off my bloodstained clothes, took a hot shower and wrapped a soft bathrobe around my energized body before returning to the bedroom, surprised to find Aidan was still here. Upon seeing me, he jumped up from the canapé and reached me in three long strides. His arms went around my waist as he pulled me closer.

"I know this is hard for you," he whispered in my ear. His voice was low and soothing, a sweet caress like his fingers against my skin.

I nodded and inhaled his scent, muttering, "You've no idea."

"Trust me, it'll get easier with time." If his words were meant to comfort me then they failed big time. But I nodded nonetheless, letting him think it was working. "I'll stay with you no matter what, Amber."

"Then prove it." I had never let him kiss me after feeding because I was ashamed of my body's need for blood when he could go without it now. Even though he had fed for centuries before the ritual freed him from his unnatural longing, I somehow felt beneath him now.

"How? You know I'd do anything to make you believe me," he whispered so low his words were almost lost in the muffled noise of Morganefaire's daily business carrying over through the open window.

"The worst thing about blood is that you can never wash away its scent, no matter how hard you try." I smiled bitterly. "But you know that since you lived like I do." He nodded. His gaze betrayed his uncertainty as to where this was heading. I grabbed his hand and pulled him toward the bed, then forced him down next to me. "I want you to see the dark side of me."

My mouth found his and our lips touched. He flinched slightly at the metallic scent on my tongue. My hand moved to the back of his nape and pressed gently. Aidan pulled back and his gaze locked on me.

His fingers touched my lips and a tiny spark flew between us. He smiled lazily.

"Did you think I'd head for the nearest door at the outlook of a bit of blood on your skin?" His blue eyes sparkled with something. Danger, determination, defiance, I couldn't tell. "You can try me all you want. I'm up for the challenge, Amber. I hope you can handle what you've unleashed."

I barely got enough time to draw a sharp breath before his lips found me again in a earthshattering kiss. My body melt into his as my brain went foggy. And then the ground beneath my feet began to spin and I was lost in Aidan's heated embrace and the sweet touch of his hands on my skin.

Chapter 14

I spent the rest of the day rummaging through my wardrobe like a headless chicken, tossing clothes out, then back in, only to go through them one more time. For someone who had thought of packing for every opportunity, I found I completely forgot to pack for a night out in the cold, patrolling the streets like an invisible shadow, while most sane people were sleeping soundly in their beds.

"All black, babe. You need to blend in with the night. That's about the first rule of the Night Guard," Aidan said from the divan near the bed, his lips twitching as usual when he found me particularly strange or amusing, or both.

"What?" I feigned surprise. "You mean my red sparkly dress and stilettos won't work?"

He laughed. "Definitely not. No heels."

"Why not?" I shrugged. "I can run faster than you in a pair of heels. You see, I have impeccable balance."

"I've seen your *impeccable balance*...without heels."

"It's a stupid rule if you ask me," I muttered, frustrated. "This is the only black top I have." I tossed a sleeveless, sheer piece of nothing toward him. He caught it in mid-air and spread it out in front of him.

"Uh, no." He grimaced. "In fact, you're not wearing this outside the house, or I might just have to fend off your countless admirers trying to break down the door to get a date with you."

I smiled and leaned in to plant a quick kiss across his gorgeous lips. "Thank you. You're too cute."

He put the shirt aside, probably planning to burn it later so I wouldn't wear it outside, and came to his feet, his gaze narrowing on me. "I'll meet you downstairs at dusk. Please don't be late."

Waving him out, I assured him I wouldn't be. Unfortunately, something else came in between: Julie.

Aidan was barely out for a minute and I breathed out, happy to be able to focus on choosing the right clothes when a voice squealed with delight, startling me. "You have so many clothes. Can I try them on? The white dress's just gorgeous. You'd never find anything like that in Morganefaire."

I didn't even look up. "If you haven't noticed already, I'm kind of facing a fashion disaster here."

"Spill." She hovered a few inches above my bed, the usual black fog gathering beneath her.

"I'm joining the Night Guard." Only after catching her expression did I realize my blunder. "It's for investigative purposes," I hurried to add.

"Oh, okay." Her stance relaxed a little, but not fully. "So, they offered you the position?"

I shook my head vehemently. "No, of course not. Aidan knows someone, who got him in. He's checking out what's going on, so he asked me to join him because he worries about leaving me behind." It was half the truth. Aidan worried a lot about me, but I'm sure he would've felt better if I stayed behind, locked up in my room. Julie's lips curled into a wide smile and her expression brightened again. The little white lie was definitely worth it.

"And you're looking for something to wear? I think I can help." Without waiting for an invitation she jumped up and glided over to flick through my wardrobe, muttering, "Nope. Urgh. Yeah, not so much. Maybe—if you were going on a hot date with your boyfriend." By the time she finished her thoughts were written all over her face. "You know Morganefaire isn't Hollywood, right?"

I snorted. "You sound like Aidan."

"He might be a bit uptight, but I think in this case he has a point." She tapped her fingers against her lips, and for the first time I realized she wasn't wearing the same nightgown as before.

"When did you change?" I asked, surprised.

"Oh, this rag." She pointed down her skinny jeans, silver tank top and black faux leather jacket. "I picked this up on my way here."

I inched closer to get a better look at the fog enveloping her feet. It wasn't as dense as before so I caught a glimpse of her open-toe, five-inch boots with tiny diamanté straps running across her ankles. "Are those designer shoes?"

"What?" Julie laughed. The squeal sounded so loud and fake, it made me want to press my hands against my ears to tune out the noise. "Do you think they are? I didn't even notice."

"But you're a ghost. I don't understand. How can you do that?"

She smiled. "I've been practicing, you see. I can touch physical stuff by concentrating really hard. It gives me a headache and I have to rest." Which must've been the reason why she disappeared right before donning a new outfit. I nodded encouragingly so she continued. "With clothes, it's a breeze. I can close my eyes and picture them on myself, and they just appear. I think I got it licked. Now giving Kieran a smooch, that's a whole different story." She pouted. "I have yet to figure out how to touch people and make them feel it."

My curiosity piqued, hundreds of questions raced through my mind. I wanted to ask where she got her outfit from and whether she could change any time, but I had other things to worry about. Time was running out. If I was late, Aidan might not mind so much but I doubted the Night Guard would wait for me to make my grand entrance.

"You know what, tell me about it later." I waved my hand. "Right now, I need something black. Anything, as long as I blend in."

"I know this place that's just perfect," Julie said. My brain screamed this was a bad idea, that I should ask Aidan to teleport back home and get me something from my own closet, or go myself, and yet I kept quiet. For one, Aidan was busy and I didn't want to burden him with my tiny and meaningless problems. And second, sneaking out of Morganefaire without telling him was out of the question. Besides, Julie seemed so enthusiastic about the whole idea, I just couldn't break her heart. Okay, I admit those were just excuses because I missed going shopping with my girlfriends and I was very curious about what Morganefaire had to offer in terms of retail therapy.

"We'll have to be quick," I said, grabbing my purse and heading out the door.

Julie walked past and took charge, hurrying me through the narrow cobblestone streets. The evening sun hid behind thick rainclouds. A few people were hurrying home, probably eager to barricade themselves inside their houses before darkness fell. After a brief, hastened walk we reached a side door.

"Are you sure this is it?" I asked unconvinced. The gray building with closed shutters looked like it hid a felon or two. Being a vampire came with unnatural strength and what else not, but I had yet to learn the tricks. I didn't want to go in there and risk being kidnapped and offered up for ransom.

"Loosen up," Julie said. "I swear you're slowly turning into Aidan. Now, come on in." I didn't want to point out she only knew Aidan and me for less than forty-eight hours. I tried the door and to my surprise found it unlocked. Julie breezed past me, so I had no choice than to follow her.

Chapter 15

From outside, the building looked like it belonged to a gang but once inside I realized everything was clean and tidy. The back door led into a spacious hall with tiny windows that barely let any daylight through. Thick gray curtains parted the space into various partitions with racks full of clothes. Chairs, makeup tables and mirrors lined the walls to the left and right. My boots thumping across the naked floor, I walked from partition to partition, trying to figure out what this place reminded me of. And then the answer dawned on me: the backstage of a theater. My breath caught in my throat.

"Julie," I hissed. "What the heck? You said you knew the perfect shop. You can't have me enter a theater without permission."

She rolled her eyes at me. "Uh, no, I never said *shop*. I said I knew the perfect *place*. You've got to admit I was right." She smoothed out her outfit and smiled. "This is where I picked up my jacket. Isn't it gorgeous? I used to get all my clothes from here before, you know—" she cleared her throat "—things happened."

My jaw dropped. "You didn't."

She grinned, all white teeth flashing. "I did!"

I felt like slapping my forehead or, better yet, slap *her*. "It's illegal."

"Who's going to catch me?" She smiled diabolically. "See, that's one of the perks of being a spirit."

"It's still illegal," I said. "I'm going home."

She stepped in front of me, blocking my way. "Don't be such a wuss. Like you've never done anything illegal in your life."

That kind of shut me up. I did a few things. The worst one yet was sneaking into a hut in the woods and taking a bag of worthless jewels that belonged to the ruler of the Lore Court, Layla, just because my brother insisted he had been watching the hut for weeks and no one lived there. Not only did it grant me my necromancy gift, it also had half the paranormal world hunt me down.

"I'm still leaving," I said, walking past her. "Last time I went down this road it only ended in complete and utter disaster. I learned my lesson the hard way." Julie swooshed toward the door and slammed it in my face. The walls reverberated from the impact. I cocked a brow, unimpressed. "Nice trick. You're learning a lot out here on your own. From trial and error or did someone give you tips?"

"You're not going anywhere," Julie hissed. I peered at her shiny eyes in horror, almost expecting her to turn into a demon. "If you don't blend in, they'll never let you join them and you'll never solve my murder. I swear if you mess this up, I'll haunt you for the rest of your life. And it won't be pretty." Something in her tone told me she meant every word of it. I hesitated. If I caved in, Julie might start thinking her threats worked on me. If I didn't do as she demanded, she might just decide to haunt me indeed. I couldn't live with a ghost breathing down my neck.

"Don't go," Julie begged. "I'm not always such a moody pants but I'm trying to hide the pain that I may never go to Heaven or Hell—or anywhere at all. I don't want to just drift around here for eternity. No one can hear me. I have yet to meet another ghost. It gets lonely."

Her lips quivered, her hands gathered in her lap, twisting the hem of her shirt nervously. Now this was worse than anger because I didn't know how to deal with it or what to expect next. I regarded her intently as I tried to figure out whether she was putting on a show. Her expression remained earnest, the pain in her eyes real. Oh, for crying out loud! If she was lying, I was falling for it big time, and I couldn't even help myself. I didn't want her to be trapped forever. "I won't let that happen to you, Julie," I said softly as I inched closer.

She clapped her hands, her expression brightening instantly. "Then let's get down to business because we're on the clock. There's tons of stuff to choose from. You'll be spoiled for choice."

I shook my head in disbelief at her sudden mood change, too sick of it to start an argument. "Fine," I said. "But I'm paying for everything. And—" I raised a finger to stop her from interrupting me "—once we're done I'm bringing everything back, cleaned and ironed, or so." I might just skip the last part because ironing wasn't really my thing. It wasn't a matter of not enjoying it, but somehow, as my brief period of working for Aidan proved, irons didn't particularly like me and managed to burn everything in their wake, including my fingers.

"Deal," Julie said. "Follow me. I know my way around. Basically, this is my second home." Why didn't I doubt that? I didn't even get a chance to ask what she meant because she continued her monologue. "I always wanted to be an actress, a dancer, and a singer, and used to perform here once a week."

I watched her happy face and smiled. "A triple threat."

"I can't help that I was born with this much talent." She grimaced, good-humored, and remained silent for a moment, giving me a chance to look at the racks filled with clothes of all shapes and sizes. As

Julie skimmed through them, I walked a step behind her, growing more and more exasperated with myself for letting a ghost bully me into agreeing to do something as stupid as this. Of course a theater wouldn't have the kind of clothes you'd need to blend in with the Night Guard, but Julie didn't seem to agree.

"Anyway," Julie resumed her chatter, a sadness permeating her voice, "wouldn't it be awesome to travel around the world and perform in Broadway plays? I wanted to do it all, from musicals and comedies to Shakespeare, and maybe one day even see my name in lights and work in the Big Apple. I was just waiting for my big break."

Her words sat in the pit of my stomach like a rock. I tried to ignore the sudden melancholy washing over me. "I'm sure you could do Broadway in Heaven. There's all kinds of heavenly choirs to join. At least that's what Cass told me. Her mother's an angel."

"She's sweet?"

"No." I laughed. "She's literally an angel."

"Uh-huh." Julie stopped flicking through one rack and pulled out what looked like a giant, black bed sheet or something a monk from the fourteenth century would wear, staring at it intently. I couldn't believe she was seriously considering it. After what seemed like an eternity, she put the monk gown slash bed sheet back and resumed both her search and chatter. "You know a lot of odd people."

"That I can't deny," I said.

"What about this one?" She held up a glossy, black, front zip bodysuit including a shiny belt, tight in all the wrong places, that might just look great on a diver...or a burglar. I tried to imagine myself in it, but only managed to conjure the image of a black balloon. Trust me, it wasn't a pretty sight.

"I couldn't possibly wear that. Have you seen my hips?"

Julie inclined her head and tapped a finger against her lips. "Hmm, you're right."

"You could've at least pretended I wasn't right," I muttered under my breath.

"What about this one?" She pointed at a baggy white jumpsuit at least four sizes too big. It looked like a painter's outfit, minus the splashes of paint. It was even more horrendous than the black bodysuit.

"In case you haven't noticed, it's white! That tiny detail might just not help me blend in very well."

Julie shrugged. "We could dye it."

"Are you mad? We have to be back in an hour. That's not enough time to dye an oversized piece of cotton. Not to mention it looks like a shapeless sack of potatoes."

"It's not my fault nothing fits you." She crossed her arms over her chest and shot me a venomous look. "I was just trying to help, you know."

I took a deep breath to calm myself. "I know. I'm sorry. Just let me do this, please."

"Fine," she said, but the edge in her voice told me she was nothing but fine with it. Ignoring her, I took a good five minutes to go through rack after rack of clothes in the hope I might find *something* that wasn't hideous, ludicrous, or downright cringeworthy. In the end I decided Julie probably picked the best pieces.

"I'll take the diver's outfit," I heard myself say.

"Told you. Besides, it's supposed to be Catwoman." Julie smiled triumphantly and tossed it toward me. I caught it in mid-air and tried not to look at it as I pushed it inside my handbag, lest I change my mind, then fished out a handful of coins and left them on one of the makeup tables.

When we left the theater the evening sky was streaked with red and orange. Hurrying through the streets, we reached home in the nick of time to get changed, toss my red coat over my outfit, and slip into a flat pair of boots. Outside, dawn slowly descended and dark gray clouds shooed away the burning colors of the evening. I waited until Aidan and Kieran closed the shutters before I joined them in the hall. Thank Goodness they didn't switch on the lights and my coat hid half of my outfit.

Kieran eyed me up and down. "That coat's going to have to go, and pronto. They'll see us from space."

"Why?" I peered down, frowning. "What's wrong with it?"

"Are you kidding me?" Kieran laughed. "You look like a big neon advertisement with the inscription, Hey, everyone, we're over here. Just follow the big red target." He raised his brows at Aidan. "Didn't you fill her in on what to wear?"

"You know Amber has a mind of her own," Aidan muttered. Damn straight.

"I was cold," I said, raising my chin defiantly. "But don't worry I'll take it off. I'll meet you guys outside, okay?"

Aidan shot me a questioning look but didn't argue. I waited until the door closed behind them, then slipped out of my beautiful red coat.

"They have no sense for fashion," Julie said with a sigh full of regret.

I nodded and headed out, wondering what they'd say once they saw my Catwoman outfit.

The street was empty, the shutters closed for the night. Hundreds of stars dotted the night sky. The torch in front of our house had not been lit yet, or maybe it had been blown out. For a moment, I honestly hoped the guys wouldn't notice, but then Aidan frowned.

"Now we're talking," Kieran said with a leer. I thought he might just start to wolf-whistle or something.

"Oh, shut up." I walked past when Aidan grabbed my arm to stop me.

"You took the whole afternoon looking for clothes and *that's* what you decided to wear?"

I shrugged and rolled my eyes. "You said anything black and no exposed skin. This covers my entire body."

"You look hot," Kieran chimed in. "And very distracting. No wonder they don't let women join the Night Guard."

"It was Julie's idea," I said.

"So not true," Julie yelled in my ear. "Tell them you're lying." I shook my head. "Tell them!" she yelled again.

"Fine," I said for the sake of my hearing. "She wants me to tell you that I'm lying. I agreed to wear the costume, but only because I don't have anything else to wear."

"Nice." Kieran winked. "I bet the remaining accessories are hidden in your bedroom."

"I don't know what you're talking about," I said, ignoring him.

"Tell him that I could wear this for him," Julie yelled in my ear. "And that I'd look hot in it."

I groaned inwardly, ignoring her also. Both of them were as annoying as flies with an inflated ego you couldn't fit through the door. They were so conceited I swear they'd just hit it off. Too bad Kieran wasn't a necromancer.

"You know, I could put on my pantomime outfit and we could go as twins," Kieran said, bursting in a fit of laughter.

I took off down the street, hoping they'd leave me alone but, as usual, that was too much to ask for.

"Where did you get it from anyway?" Kieran asked. "It looks like something on television in a late night show, you know, the one not suitable for watchers under eighteen."

"You'd know." I shot him a peeved look.

"Unfortunately, my brother's right for a change. Put on my coat," Aidan said, slipping out of it to reveal a black shirt that hung to his body like a sheath. For once, I didn't argue. His leather coat weighed a ton and was a few sizes too large, but it smelled of him and made Kieran shut up. I inhaled slowly to soothe my nerves, only now realizing my hands were shaking. We had a mission to fulfill. I didn't know what to expect, but I could feel its magnitude in the air. Julie seemed to sense it too because she glided beside us in silence as we made our way to the designated meeting point at the northwest side of the wall.

Chapter 16

Thunder broke the silence. A light drizzle covered my face; tiny drops at first that soon turned into torrential rain flooding the darkened streets of Morganefaire. The rain was so strong my eyelashes clung to my cheeks and made me waddle around blindly. I stepped easily over the slick bricks, minding Aidan's leather coat that seemed to want to soak up every drop of water in the surrounding area, and hurried my pace to keep up with Aidan and Kieran.

"We're close to the wall," Aidan said.

I swallowed hard. So this was supposed to be the stuff of my nightmares. If only I could see a darn thing.

Kieran touched my shoulder to get my attention. "Hey, now would be as good a time as any."

"What?" I yelled through the thunder rumbling overhead.

"To show us the hot outfit you're wearing."

"But I'm soaked." And then I understood his suggestion. The idiot wanted to see some kind of wet T-shirt contest. I rolled my eyes. "Get your freak on somewhere else, Kieran."

"I was just kidding." He grinned proudly. "I've got a girlfriend now."

"That certainly didn't stop you from making an unnecessary comment. Just keep moving," Aidan said. "The guys are along this border somewhere."

Lightning flashed, illuminating the towering buildings around us for a moment. "You sure you got the right spot?" Kieran asked.

"Do I look like I make mistakes?" Aidan snapped, stomping through a shallow puddle of water.

Kieran followed behind. "No. Never. Oh mighty Aidan, Lord of the Vampires."

Aidan shot him an irritated look but didn't comment. I only noticed the men of the Night Guard—around twenty-five or thirty of them—when I almost bumped into the dark-haired guy, Iain. He wrapped his arm around my waist to steady me, laughing out loud, the sound echoing in my ears and getting on my nerves. I pressed my hand against his softening belly to put some distance between us and wiped a hand over my damp eyes. The downpour calmed down a little, but not quite enough. I probably looked like a wet raccoon with streaks of mascara running down my face. Definitely not the impression I wanted to give on my first day on the job.

I shot Aidan my 'got-it-under-control' smile and turned back to Iain who seemed to have started his instructions for the night.

"We'll be around the corner, watching the east of the city. You stay here and watch this part of the wall in a five hundred feet parameter to your right," Iain called to me through the rain, pointing ahead. "You need to climb on *top* of the wall; that's what the *ladders* are for." He emphasized the words like I was an idiot.

"Amber is a badass you don't want to mess with," Kieran said. "She's up to the challenge so leaving her here is an insult I won't stand for."

Aidan nodded. "Kieran's right. There's nothing here to guard." I peered at the dark shadow that presumably was the wall rising against the canvass of the night. Behind me was nothing but buildings and empty streets stretching out in the distance. Everything looked quiet, isolated and, most importantly, boring.

"Precisely. We don't need a woman standing in our way." Iain chuckled and turned away.

I caught his arm and forced him to face me, and for a moment I felt rage bubble up inside me. "Mate, you've no idea who you're talking to," I hissed.

His Adam's apple bobbed up and down as he swallowed hard, but he didn't try to escape my iron grip. Eventually, I let go of him and turned on my heel. If he wanted me northwest of the wall, then so be it. I'd circle it once, maybe twice, then commence my own investigation. No guy would ever tell me what to do. I wondered why they wanted to recruit Julie for the Night Guard when their view on women wasn't so great, basically still stuck in medieval times. What did they want Julie for anyway? To get them coffee...or mugs of ale?

"Amber," Aidan called after me. "Wait up," he said, grabbing my arm. "I'm going to get you a better assignment. You're a force to be reckoned with."

"Damn straight," Kieran said, stepping behind him.

Aidan's lips pressed into a grim line. "We need their support but if they can't treat you as an equal, then I'm leaving."

"Me too," Kieran said to Aidan. "I told you we couldn't trust a guy in tights. Their taste in clothing is as bad as yours."

I grabbed my boyfriend's arm, my eyes throwing daggers at Iain, who was standing a few feet away to give us privacy. "No! Don't start trouble over me," I said. "You're right, we need them on our side. I can take one for the team. But if it wasn't for this brethren and war thing, I'd kick his ass into next week."

He smiled. "I'd kick him into next month."

Seeing Aidan stick up for me was so romantic and sweet, I almost forgot my anger. "For now, we'll play by his rules. I'll try to control my temper for the sake of the greater good." I gently brushed my fingertips over his lips, right where the raindrops entered his mouth, and rose on my toes to capture his mouth in a tender kiss.

"We'll be around the corner." He hesitated. I could sense the 'if you need me' part in the air. Thank goodness he kept quiet.

"Great." I turned my back on him and started in the direction Iain had pointed. For a while, I could hear the men in the distance, joking and laughing, as though their job was nothing more than a gathering of friends over the usual weekly drink. But their voices grew faint, their words indistinct, until I could hear them no more. The sound of my boots pounding the cobblestone path was almost as loud as the white noise made by the rain. And then, all of a sudden, the rain stopped and the sky cleared. The clouds made room for countless stars to take their place. Even Julie seemed to have forsaken me.

I walked five hundred feet to my right, then stopped to peer around me, wondering how it could possibly be so quiet. Even in the middle of nowhere in Scotland, the night came with its own noises: fireflies buzzing around the bushes, owls hooting for their prey, tiny critters scavenging the bushes for food. My heightened hearing usually picked up every sound, but here the night remained as silent as a tomb. Just to hear *something*, even if it was my own footsteps, and to be sure I hadn't gone completely deaf from Julie's screaming, I blew my hot breath into my palms and circled the last building until I stood in front of the imposing structure that was Morganefaire's wall.

Except for the gate on the south side, the wall formed an unbroken barricade between Morganefaire's inhabitants and the outside world. The thick bricks reached at least twenty feet into the sky and glistened in the moonlight. I didn't see a ladder, but between the stones were tiny indentations that looked like countless eyes. I guessed their purpose was to climb up because they reminded me of the protrusions used for indoor climbing walls. I pushed my index finger into one of the dents and tested the stone. My palm nestling comfortably against the opening I raised myself a few inches off the ground. It seemed secure enough and yet...my heart began to pump harder and a first rivulet of sweat trickled down my back. I swear for a moment even my head began to spin.

"No freaking way," I muttered, jumping back down. The Night Guard might not mind climbing up a wall in the middle of the night, but I wasn't going to risk my neck for nothing. Kneeling the way I had been taught, I pressed my knuckles into the ground and then jumped. I've no idea how I did it but somehow I managed to land on top of the about half a foot-wide wall without tripping, toppling over, or losing my balance.

I took a deep breath and planted my feet wide to steady myself before scanning the city of Morganefaire below. Gosh, it seemed a long way down. Heights weren't really my thing. I could only hope jumping down was as easy as jumping up, otherwise I might just have a problem.

"It's going to be okay," I mumbled to myself as I focused on the task at hand. It was like being lost in a time warp. To my left, cafes, shops and townhouses in the style of twelfth-century architecture lined the main street. To my right, a giant windmill whirled away in the breeze. Not far from it, a few stray sheep huddled together on a small picturesque field near a winding cobblestone street lined with quaint cottages, beyond which were terraced vineyards and fields. With the rain cleared, my vision amazed me; I could even see the raindrops dripping from the colorful potted flowers dotting the porches. From the corner of my eye I caught an orange spark flickering and growing into a fire as large as the trunk of a tree. In spite of its size, the darkness around it remained impenetrable.

"That's the night torch," Julie said from my left, startling me.

I jumped a step back, losing my balance for an instant. "What's wrong with you?" I hissed. "Never sneak up on people like that!"

"Why the grumpy face?" She regarded me curiously.

"For starters, I almost fell. I could've broken every bone in my body," I said.

Julie laughed, her crystalline voice echoing in the silence. "You're forgetting you're not human anymore."

I forgot indeed. "Thanks for the reminder. But just to clarify, I'm not immune to pain."

"I've never met a vampire who's afraid of her own shadow. That's funny."

"I highly doubt you ever met a vampire at all," I muttered.

She inhaled, tossed her head back, and stretched out her arms to the side Titanic-style chanting something like, "This is the life."

I couldn't agree less. "Get out of my way. I'm supposed to do a job here," I muttered. "And you're definitely not helping."

"Nope. This is *my* job and you're helping *me*, remember?"

"Fine." I inched closer, figuring she'd step aside if she thought I'd walk through her. She stood her ground.

"You're going the wrong way," Julie said.

"That's where I was told to go, five hundred feet to my right and then back to the meeting point."

Julie heaved an exaggerated sigh. "And you do everything people tell you to do?"

She had a point. Dallas told me to get a housekeeping job and retrieve some gems. I did it. Aidan instructed me to find the Book of the Dead. I did it. Cass told me to channel ghosts for her reality television program. I did it. Rebecca made me kiss another man. And I did it—well, technically, I was possessed so it doesn't really count. But you know what? I was tired of being bossed around.

If I was supposed to waste a good night's sleep out here, then I might as well have fun whilst doing so. I was missing all the action because the guys told me to, and in my book a guy ordering a woman around was unacceptable.

Shooting her a thankful smile I took off, past the five hundred feet parameter I was given. The night torch disappeared behind me as I moved north. I hurried my pace, exhilarated at the thought that I was breaking a few rules here. Even if someone caught me, there was nothing they could do. I could play the dumb chick and pretend I couldn't count to five hundred. Or, even better, I could tell them to suck it up.

A strong breeze began to shake the shutters of the buildings below. The night remained dark, illuminated only by the soft glow of the stars, until we reached the next torch. Julie's hand wrapped around my wrist, sending an electric jolt through me.

"We're near the north side," she whispered, as though she feared being overheard. "This is where the torch went out."

It all looked just the same to me. I frowned as I peered at her pale face. "Why isn't a guard stationed here? Shouldn't there be one every five hundred feet?"

"Every one thousand," Julie said. "He never turned up yesterday, and today he doesn't seem to want to be here either."

"That's strange. Do you think something scared him?"

Julie shrugged. "I don't know, but Morganefaire's guards never abandon their positions, no matter what. They took an oath to protect the city."

Foul play? "We should go back and inform the others."

I turned on my heel when Julie stopped me, whispering, "Listen. Do you hear that?"

I nodded, only now noticing the scratching sound coming from outside the city walls directly beneath me. It was faint, barely audible, and yet unmistakably there. Probably some animal or small rodent sharpening its claws. "What *is* that?"

"The hands I told you about," Julie whispered. "If you lean over the wall far enough you can see them."

A shiver ran down my spine. Crawling hands were so not my thing. Even though I didn't really believe in them, I felt compelled to look. Kneeling down, I tilted my head over the edge, but not far enough to topple over.

"Do you see them?" Julie whispered in my ear.

I craned my neck to get a better glimpse at the darkness below. "Not a single finger." My lips curled into a smile. The people here were so superstitious they'd make every fanatic cult rich beyond their wildest dreams.

"A vampire with a bad sense of humor," she muttered. "You're just in denial."

"Seriously?"

She raised her chin defiantly. "They're there. Everyone knows that."

I nodded slowly. Another grin tugged at my lips. "Yeah. Without a doubt."

Something flickered in Julie's gaze. Hot waves of anger wafted from her. Yet another ghostly mood swing coming my way. I figured I'd better take cover before it hit me. "Let's go," I said, standing.

"You're not going anywhere," Julie hissed. Before I even realized what was happening, her hands moved through me, grabbing and shoving with such force I stumbled backward. It was just a tiny step but enough to trip over my own feet. Flapping my hands about to grab onto something, I felt the ground disappear beneath my feet.

And then I fell.

Chapter 17

No matter what movies tell you, vampires can't turn into bats and they certainly don't possess the ability to fly. What they can, however, is hold on for dear life. I was the living proof. Okay, *dead* proof, but you get the point.

As Julie pushed me off the wall and the solid ground disappeared from under my feet, my arms flailing around me, my fingers miraculously managed to grab the edge. My legs bounced in mid-air, trying to find something to hold onto and heave myself up, but my attempts remained futile. This side of the wall was as smooth as ice.

"Get someone," I said.

"You act like you're in trouble. As if. Embrace your immortal DNA. It shouldn't be that hard."

My hand strained to hold my weight, but I didn't know how much longer I could hold on. "Be quiet for a change and help me."

"Or what?"

"Or I'm calling a light worker, or priest—whatever gets rid off you," I yelled at her.

"What's a light worker?" Julie asked, unimpressed.

"A case worker for ghosts."

"Oh." She giggled, obviously not taking me very seriously. "Just climb over."

My boots glided across the wall ungracefully. I probably looked like someone having their first ice skating lesson, only on a vertical surface. It was beyond weird, not to mention embarrassing. "I can't. There's nothing to hold onto."

"Morganefaire magic's a bitch, huh?" Julie kept staring at me, not moving from the spot.

I peered below. It seemed like the impenetrable darkness stretched out for hundreds of feet. I might physically survive a fall into that bottomless pit, but my ego wouldn't. With my crappy luck, the Night Guard might just find me flat on my butt. And that wouldn't be good because half the paranormal world was already laughing at me. The other half might just join in soon if I couldn't even patrol a wall without taking a tumble. Of course it wasn't even my mistake, but who'd believe me a whacky ghost pushed me?

"Julie, stop just floating around and get Aidan," I hissed.

"He can't see me." She sighed. "This is all your fault. What sort of vampire are you if you can't even keep your balance?"

Grimacing, I forced myself to keep quiet because arguing with a ghost was useless, not to mention a waste of time. Instead of calling the priest I kept threatening her with, I merely smiled in a beatific sort of way, thinking how soon all these things would be inconsequential to me, basically part of a distant memory, alongside saving humanity from Rebecca's gathering vampire hordes. I had to focus on coming up with a plan to climb back up before a guard found me. My second hand moved up but my fingers couldn't grab onto the wall. It was as though the stone turned to ice beneath my grip, and it felt just as cold. I had never seen or heard of this kind of magic before, but it certainly scared the hell out of me.

Julie sat down and bounced her legs over the edge as though she had no care in the world. "Do you see them now?"

"See what?" I tried to keep my annoyance out of my tone, but it was hard.

"The hands."

"Oh, the hands!" I smirked. "That's why I'm risking a few broken bones, to see some freaking hands that don't even exist!" Her eyes glimmered with anger again. I had to tread carefully, or she might just decide to do something even more stupid than shoving me.

A scratching sound carried over from below. I peered into the darkness, but saw nothing. And then the noise started again, only this time it seemed to come from several spots and didn't stop.

It had to be mice, my brain argued. Nothing else made sense. When Rebecca haunted me inside Aidan's house, she had made similar sounds. But I doubted I had another poltergeist activity on my hands since poltergeists don't bother you outside of buildings. Rodents was the only reasonable explanation I could come up with.

My gaze was glued to the black pit beneath my feet. Something pale shimmered in the moonlight, then disappeared, only to appear again a second later. I swallowed hard and tried to avert my eyes, but for some reason my curiosity kept me both petrified and fascinated at the same time. I squinted and focused until I could make out the shape of a hand with long fingers, distorted in places so it didn't even look human any more. It stretched up, fingers coiling and recoiling, as though reaching to grab me. Thank goodness the ground was a long way down.

A second hand appeared, then a third, and so on, until the ground below was covered in limbs that shimmered in the night, swaying softly as they clenched and unclenched, reminding me of a macabre dance. Whatever those were, no way was I falling in there and letting them touch me or drag me to hell, buried alive beside them. The thought sent a cold shudder down my spine.

I swallowed hard and held onto the edge tighter. "Julie, get someone *now*," I said. "There's something down there."

"Told you," Julie said, triumphantly.

"Just shut up and help me. If those things touch me you'll have a very pissed necromancer on your hands." I huffed as I tried to grab hold of the edge with my dangling hand, and failed...for the umpteenth time. "Do you know what'll happen to your sorry ass? I'll channel your ghost into one of those things below and leave you trapped in there for a month. How about that?"

"That's not fair," she screeched, giving me a headache. "What am I supposed to do?" She stood from her sitting position and peered around her. The ghost was as useless as she was annoying. In the end, she just reached out, as though to clutch my arm. "Give me your hand and I'll try to pull you up."

"What?" I snorted. "No way. You've been a ghost for a whole two days and might've figured out how to blow out a few candles and open a door, but I'm not trusting you with my *life*."

"I can do it."

Not only was she annoying, she was also delusional. But what other choice did I have? "Fine."

I raised my dangling arm to hers. She hesitated, which wasn't a good sign. As she leaned forward, her face scrunched up in concentration. Her fingers touched mine...and ran right through me, sending a jolt through my arm that was so strong I almost lost my grip.

"Sorry," she muttered.

"Just do it again," I said through gritted teeth.

She nodded and tried again. The jolt was stronger than before, but this time I felt something else: a tremor followed by a hard push. My heart almost skipped a beat. In that fragment of a second I thought my body was gone and I was floating in a giant void surrounded by *nothingness*. I no longer felt the wind caressing the physical sheath of my mortal body and the stars above were gone, just like the wall. Even my own heart was gone.

"Julie!" I hissed. "Stop it."

Returning from that sense of nonexistence, I blinked and shook my head slightly to make sure it was still there. The thought of floating around in that abyss had me paralyzed with fear. It was even enough to make me forget the wobbling hands beneath my feet.

"Sorry. Didn't work," Julie said. "One more time, okay?" The stupid ghost was about to possess me and didn't even notice.

"No!" I yelled. "You almost possessed me!"

Her face dropped and her eyes widened. "Oh." A glimmer appeared in her gaze, followed by...pride? I groaned. She couldn't be serious. "I really did?" she asked.

"Hey, focus on getting me back up there," I snapped. Countless ideas as to what I'd do with her once I got my hands on her entered my head.

"Take it down a notch because it's not like you're human or anything. I mean if you were you'd be splattered across the rocks like a smashed watermelon...that is, if you even survived the 'hands'." She glanced down into my eyes. "You're an immortal being, Amber. Use your immortal tricks."

I was still a newbie, for crying out loud. Why didn't people get that part? "I might have immortal strength to hang on but Morganefaire magic's making the wall slick like ice." As though the wall heard me, it turned a tiny bit smoother. Filled with horror, I watched my fingers slowly starting to lose their grip. Sweat poured down my back. For one minute, I considered shouting for help but what would the others think? I couldn't tamper with Aidan's reputation.

She hovered a few inches above the edge and tapped her fingers against the thigh. "Why don't you just do that disappearing act Kieran keeps doing?"

"What disappearing act?"

"I've been watching him. He dissolves into thin air at night," Julie said. "He returns in the morning before your boyfriend wakes up."

My mind put two and two together. Kieran was teleporting somewhere, but I had no time to ponder his whereabouts because Julie was spot-on. I could just imagine myself standing on top of the wall and, thanks to my vampiric abilities, I'd be transported through time and space to the desired spot. Why didn't I think of trying that before?

I focused on the few images etched into my mind: the old worn out stone weathered by snow and rain and Julie's open-toe, five-inch boots with tiny diamanté straps running across her ankles in a black cloud swirling underneath her. Trying to remember every single detail I could so I wouldn't end up a frozen iceberg in Alaska, I added tiny flecks of limestone granite to the wall. That would be my focal point so I could tune into my immortal power locked away deep inside. I took a deep breath and closed my eyes as I forced my mind to conjure the image. The air began to shift around me, making my stomach coil. My grip around the stone loosened. The next thing I knew I felt solid ground beneath my feet.

"It worked," Julie squealed, almost sending me back over the edge again.

"It did." I laughed with her. "Thank you. I thought I was going to break a few bones down there."

"Or worse." She pointed in the distance at a shadow, darker than the night, moving toward us at a fast speed. The sky above it looked like a giant hole; air seemed to whirl like a tornado that bathed everything in its wake in pitch black.

"It's just a bit of wind, right?" In spite of my words, I moved a step back.

"Not quite." A pause. Then, "You know, maybe we should get down from here." She didn't even wait for my reply. With a last glance over her shoulder, she floated down the wall and onto the paved street below.

My gaze drifted to the sea of hands that almost gobbled me up. They were there, scratching away at the wall in their fruitless attempt to get inside the city. I couldn't believe I didn't see them before.

"Are you coming or what?" Julie whispered. Jumping, I landed on my feet right next to her. I opened my mouth to speak when she raised her finger to her lips to shush me. "Listen."

I followed her command. For a minute I heard nothing, and then the wailing began, growing louder and louder as it inched closer. I say 'wailing' because it faintly reminded me of hundreds of voices calling and bawling their eyes out, but in truth I had never heard anything like it before. Cold shudders ran up and down my spine and the hairs on my neck prickled.

"What is that?" I whispered.

"The *real* reason why people barricade themselves inside their homes at night," Julie explained. "We're not safe here and no one will open their door to let us in."

"Like this thing couldn't get inside if it wanted!" I said.

"We need to seek shelter now," she said, starting down the street. "Every building...house, shop, church...whatever...is protected by magic. The thing is forbidden to enter, but if it manages to catch you outside then it's a completely different story and all bets are off. Either you kill yourself or it kills you. Usually, it prefers the latter, slow and painful. It doesn't come out every night, but when it does, then it's every guard for himself."

My boots clanked on the stone as I hurried to keep up with her. "I don't get why you're so scared. You're a ghost."

She shook her head. "It doesn't matter. It can suck me up, too, trap me in there for eternity. As long as I'm inside a building the magic protects me whether I'm dead or not." She pointed at a wooden structure that looked like an oversized container, about a foot tall, with a latch. "Let's take cover in there."

I nodded and hurried over, then pried the latch open and jumped inside, closing it behind us.

The confined space was bathed in darkness and reeked of rotten apples and what else not but, according to Julie, it would do.

"Now, zip it," she commanded. "It will be here soon."

I tried to take shallow, silent breaths as I peered through a tiny split in the wall. The night torch on the other side of the road barely broke the darkness. Nothing stirred on the narrow street. And then I felt the first shudder in the air, a slow wave of despair and hunger that washed over me and left a strong feeling of hopelessness behind. A creepy urge to start crying ran through me and moisture gathered in my eyes.

"Don't listen to it. If you do, you'll die," Julie whispered. I wasn't going to and yet—

The black column of air appeared in my line of vision, twisting and twirling like a tornado as it made its way through the narrow street, reaching almost as high as the buildings. A violent wind tilted the trees, ready to pull them out by their roots. The buildings around us began to shake from the debris and rocks flying against the walls and the hailstones pelting against the windows. For a minute, I covered my ears to tune out the noise reminding me of hundreds of freight trains rumbling on top of me. It was the most interesting yet frightening thing I'd ever seen in my life. The wailing intensified and grew into a crescendo. Even our container started to vibrate and shake. I could only hope we were safe.

Peeking out, I stared at the black column moving closer. Leading it was a naked man sitting on a stallion with bloody gashes covering his entire body. His long brown hair tied in a ponytail barely swayed in the strong breeze, as though the wind didn't have any effect on him. Sensing I was watching him, his head snapped in my direction and his hollow skeleton eyes turned on me. Blood began to drip from his mouth in tiny rivulets. Ever so slowly, his jaw opened to reveal shark-like teeth. My heart lurched when I realized that was no man. It was evil personified. I scooted up against the wall, my body trembling, and yet I couldn't stop staring.

More faces popped up in the dark spiral. Their ashen faces shimmered in the darkness as they marched along the paved street, the wind barely covering their naked bodies. They multiplied before my eyes, until the whole street was lined up with the undead army, mouths agape with despair, crying, calling, searching for something the hollow pits that once were their eyes couldn't see.

When the first skeleton face appeared only inches away from our hiding place, I thought I'd jump out of my skin. I pressed my palm against my mouth to keep me from yelping and bit hard on my tongue to stay focused.

I don't know how long Julie and I hid inside the wooden box, too petrified to move or even breathe but, after what felt like an eternity, the creepy wind passed and silence ensued. Eventually, Julie signaled that we could leave. I opened the lid and climbed out, too shaken to utter a word. Hundreds of questions raced through my mind, but none made it past my trembling lips.

"It won't come back," Julie whispered. "Not tonight." I nodded when movement on the other side of the road caught my eye. Turning my head sharply, I dived back down behind the wooden box and scanned the area.

A tall figure with a black cape disappeared around the corner, leaving a bundle behind. Realizing it was a human shape I jumped to my feet and hurried over to help. But I could tell from the darkening aura around the body that the person was already dead.

"Her name's Samantha," Julie said, her voice barely louder than a whisper. "She's a witch. You can tell by the star and moon tattoo on her left wrist."

Chapter 18

Another body in Morganefaire. Only this time, I had the luck to find it. My breath came in ragged heaps as I turned the bundle on the ground around to search for a pulse...and found none. The last time I held a body in my arms, it was my brother's, right after Rebecca attacked him in Hell because he happened to be in the wrong place at the wrong time. His soul was reunited with his body eventually, but the experience left me marked for life because I had never felt so powerless. Seeing the motionless girl at my feet, I felt similar—only this time I knew no voodoo priestess would be here to raise her from the dead.

My hands trembled; my heart beat so fast I thought my chest might explode. I had to call the others but my legs wouldn't budge from the spot. Where was the soul? Had the reaper arrived to get her and I never saw him?

"Is she dead?" Julie's eyes grew wide.

I nodded slowly.

"But—" Her lips quivered.

My gaze remained glued to the bundle on the ground. For a moment I thought I saw something shimmer beneath the thin material of her white nightgown. With shaking fingers I bared her right shoulder to reveal a raw, red spot, about the size of an almond. My finger moved across it gently, probing the indentation.

"What is that?" Julie asked, inching closer.

"I think someone removed a bit of skin," I whispered.

"I'm going to be sick." Julie suppressed a genuine gag.

"Come on." I tried to grab her arm, for a moment forgetting Julie was just a ghost, then pulled back when I realized my mistake.

"Amber?" Aidan's deep voice echoed through the night. I started off down the street to meet him halfway and jumped into his arms. A sob escaped my throat. "Are you okay?" he whispered.

I shook my head and let his presence envelop me, only now noticing the few men of the Night Guard standing behind him.

"What happened?" Aidan asked, his hands rubbing my arms gently.

"There's a body. I saw someone move it." My voice came low and hoarse. I cleared my throat to get rid of the quiver in it. The magnitude of my words sank onto me. I hadn't just discovered the body but also saw the murderer. Granted, it was only his cape, but at least I could tell it was someone tall and sturdy.

"Where?" Logan asked.

I pointed around the corner to where I had left the bundle behind. Aidan's fingers wrapped around my hand and pulled me with him as he followed the Night Guard.

***

Aidan was standing behind me, his fingers caressing my hips as I leaned into him. His muscular body, dressed in loose-fit jeans and a shirt, shielded me from the cold night wind that had started to blow. Kieran stood to my right. His black hair swayed slightly. His blue eyes shimmered like the dark ocean.

"I request a Council meeting, right here, right now," a man said. Aidan's heartbeat accelerated against my back but he remained quiet.

"Agreed," Logan said, then silence ensued as several guards disappeared to get whoever was supposed to be the Council. At least ten to fifteen minutes passed before more people arrived, among them a woman. I craned my neck to get a look at her face. Elyssa—for a moment I was fooled to believe it was her, until I noticed that her hair was shorter and her face slightly haggard, as though she didn't eat enough. She seemed older than Elyssa, too. Maybe it was her mother or an elder sister.

"Who's that?" I whispered to Aidan.

"That's Corinna. She's a member of the Council." His voice trailed off. I didn't need him to elaborate to know she wasn't on our side. Her furious expression said more than a thousand words.

One of the men spoke to her. She nodded, her gaze still focused on me. Was she blaming me for the girl's death? It sure looked like it. The guards began to chatter animatedly, then made room for the Council to gather: Iain, Logan, Corinna, Riley, an older guy called Morres and what looked like a younger version of him, Rowan.

Somewhere at the periphery of my mind, I knew what they were saying was of great importance, and yet all I could think of was the witch at our feet: so small, so frail, so...dead. It was a bit like, wherever I went, death followed. I couldn't help the sudden dread and suspicion washing over me. And who could blame me? Hadn't Aidan claimed Morganefaire was the safest place on earth? And what about all my new friends, who seemed to encounter this or that tiny inconvenience, like my brother dying and his soul having to be reunited with his body? Or voodoo priestess, Sofia, a close friend of mine, almost being sacrificed at the hands of a demi-god Seth slash her ex-boyfriend Gael. The coincidences were slowly beginning to pile up that I sort of stopped believing in accidents. I might not be a connoisseur of the paranormal world, and certainly not of Morganefaire, but my gut feeling told me this was no coincidence.

And when my gut feeling jumped in, it had a better success rate than *Google Maps*.

"When was the last time you had a series of murders in Morganefaire?" I croaked, my hand pressed against my racing heart. The guards fell instantly silent. Countless heads snapped in my direction, curiosity and mistrust mirrored in their eyes. I almost took a step back to hide behind the next night torch, even though that wasn't my style. For one second, I wished I could take my question back, but then I remembered I was innocent. I had nothing to hide. So I took a deep breath and met one furious face after another.

"We're not supposed to address the Council until they address us first," Aidan whispered in my ear.

I turned to regard him and caught a glimpse of his gloomy expression before he decided to hide it from me. "Huh? I'm not allowed to ask a question? Ever heard of democracy and freedom of speech?"

The corners of his lips twitched and a glint appeared in his eyes.

"Someone's just asked a question, and a fairly good one at that," Kieran called out.

"The last time a vampire visited," Corinna said to me. "As I'm sure you're well aware of."

"This is a Council matter. Amber's our guest and not aware of Flavius's doings," Logan said. The woman's voice pressed into a tight line. Surrounded by the men of the Night Guard, whose gaze never left me, Logan kneeled down to inspect the body as we watched in silence. My gaze remained glued to the girl's shoulder, expecting to see the mark the moment he pulled her nightgown down to reveal her neck. But it was gone. Eventually Logan got up and declared, "She's been dead for a while."

I shook my head. "That's not possible. I just saw her with the murderer."

"You probably saw him transporting her back to her sleeping quarters," Iain said.

The idea never even crossed my mind, but it certainly made sense. Or why else wouldn't the girl's ghost be around, waiting for the reaper to transport her to the Otherworld? She must have died elsewhere.

"What exactly did you see?" Iain asked. Aidan squeezed my hand, signaling I had to tread carefully. As things stood, we still had no idea who was involved in this mess. Moistening my lips, I carefully considered my words.

"I saw a figure carrying a bundle and hurried over because I sensed something was terribly wrong. The man noticed me and dropped the body before taking off. I only caught a glimpse of his cape." I decided to leave out the part about the skin. Even though the rest of my explanation was the truth, it didn't seem to please Iain, as though he knew I kept something to myself.

"No one wears a cape in Morganefaire," he said. "So, the killer dropped the body when they saw you?" I nodded, noticing he refrained from giving the murderer a gender. "Where's Blake? He's a member of the Council as well, or is he not?" Iain continued. The men began to murmur. Aidan's stance stiffened. He signaled Kieran over and whispered something in his ear.

"I'm taking Amber home," Kieran proclaimed, his tone leaving no room for discussion. Iain nodded.

"Get some rest." Logan patted my back and smiled sympathetically, like I was one of them now. I smiled back, thankful for his compassion.

Kieran grabbed my hand and shot me an imploring look. I had no intention to argue, so I followed him in silence until we turned a corner when he could no longer keep his mouth shut, "Did you see the guards' faces?" I nodded, knowing where this was leading. "Half of them wanted to chop off your head right there and then," Kieran whispered. "If it weren't for Logan being in charge and one of Aidan's friends, they might've tried just that."

"They think I'm responsible." My heart sank in my chest.

Kieran shook his head. "No, they think Blake's responsible and that you could be involved. After all, Blake wanted you here. With no blood and no clue as to what could've happened, a stranger will always be the first suspect. After spending a long time among us, Blake has become a stranger but their blood still flows through his veins. Unfortunately, it doesn't flow through yours."

I took a sharp breath as I let his words sink in. Kieran was right. The guards would soon start spreading rumors. My life was on the line. I had to be quick and solve the mystery before the residents of Morganefaire turned against me and Aidan lost their support.

"There's something I didn't tell the Council," I began slowly. Kieran's brows furrowed interested. "When I found the witch, I saw something on her shoulder: a tiny wound or mark, as though the skin was removed with a knife or a razorblade. It was beyond macabre."

"I'll tell Aidan about it," Kieran whispered.

"There's something else," I continued as I tried to keep up with his hurried pace. "Someone was supposed to guard the north side of the wall. According to Julie, the guard's been missing since yesterday."

"Why?"

I shook my head, signaling I had no idea. "He might've decided to run away like a scaredy cat. Or he was killed. Or sucked up by that wind entity."

Kieran shot me an intrigued look. "If he's alive, then maybe he saw something. Something that made him leave his post and not want to come back and tell us about it."

"You're probably right. Since we found her body in the north district and she's been dead for a while, maybe he witnessed her murder?" My mind was jumping to conclusions, but I couldn't help myself.

"Let's find out his name," Kieran said. "Who knows, we might be one step closer to discovering the murderer's identity."

His words mirrored my thoughts. "Aidan will have lots of questions once he gets home."

Chapter 19

It was past midnight when Kieran accompanied me to the door, instructed me to lock up, and then disappeared again, claiming he had some other business to attend to. In the dead silence of the house I noticed Julie was gone. Last time I saw her she was leaning over the dead witch, Samantha, inspecting the fading mark on her skin. Maybe she was too upset to talk and needed some solitude. As much as I respected her privacy, we had no time to waste.

"Julie," I called out upon entering the guest quarters. She didn't answer. I hurried from room to room, even though I knew all too well this wasn't her hiding spot. In the end, I gave up and slumped on the sofa in the living room, wondering whether to wait until she'd be back or visit the places she liked to frequent.

Waiting patiently had never been my thing. The house was so quiet and empty I refused to stay in and risk being bored to death. I shrugged into my red coat when a soft click echoed from the living room. For some inexplicable reason, I didn't think it was Julie. Beside Kieran and Aidan, there was only one more person who lived here: Maya.

The eye color change thing still haunted me. Making sure I wouldn't trip over my own two feet, I tiptoed down the hall. The curtain to the staff quarters was drawn aside. I followed the soft thud of footsteps to the back entrance and found the door unlocked. The superstitious inhabitants of Morganefaire didn't leave anything unlocked, so maybe someone forgot to lock up, or Maya ventured out into the night. But why was she still up after midnight and why would she leave the safety of her home? Unless she had something to hide. Maybe a secret lover, I mused. Or maybe she had a much darker secret.

My mistrust instantly piqued, I opened the door and stepped into the backyard in time to catch the reflection of a black shadow disappearing around the rosebushes. My mother said curiosity always got me in trouble. Maybe it did, but in this instance I felt I had no choice than to follow, so I raced after the shadow, not knowing my decision would have a disastrous outcome that would change our lives forever.

Chapter 20

A furious autumn wind began to hurl itself against Morganefaire, howling and whistling, causing the shutters of the houses to slam against the clapboards with a vigor I had rarely seen. My hair whipped against my skin as I moved through the black night at a fast speed, my mind racing ahead of me as I tried to connect the last days' events.

I thought back to Samantha and the way her body had been dragged through the darkness, swaying in the strong breeze like a dying leaf or a bed sheet on a clothing line. That was one of the more important mysteries I needed to solve. Less crucial was the question why the shadow I was following, presumably Maya, a superstitious witch who barricaded the house at night, now hurried through the empty streets at the speed of someone who had something to hide. My immortal body had no problems keeping up, but I still followed at a fifty feet distance, just to make sure she wouldn't spy me.

Was there a connection? There didn't seem to be one, and yet...I couldn't shake off the feeling that I was missing something. Of course, I could just stop Maya and ask her where she was heading. I was strong enough to *force* her to tell me the truth, if need be, but I held back. I wanted to see what was going on without raising anyone's suspicion.

This part of town seemed somehow familiar, so I wasn't surprised when Maya crossed the street and disappeared into one of the houses. I stopped in front of the building. My white reflection stared back from the window. The sign 'Bells, Books & Candles' wasn't readable in the darkness, but I didn't need to see it to know I was standing in front of Elyssa's dime store.

What was Maya doing at Elyssa's in the middle of the night? I was about to find out.

Chapter 21

The light of the street lamp cast a soft glow on the lower façade of the shop. I pushed the door hard but it didn't budge under my touch. Maya must've locked it behind her. Smart girl, but it was nothing a little teleporting couldn't fix. Closing my eyes, I imagined myself standing inside the shop, near Julie's reading spot, because I figured it was the best hiding place allowing me to supervise the entire floor. The air shifted around me, making my stomach turn. Something hard hit me and I stumbled back. Fighting the onset of nausea, I pried my eyes open only to realize I was still standing in front of Elyssa's shop. Teleporting hadn't worked. Some kind of spell must've kept me from going in, probably the same kind of magic that held me back the first time I tried to enter Bells, Books & Candles.

I needed an invitation, and quick, before someone spied me out here and called the police or medieval guards or whatever made sure the city remained orderly.

"What's up?" Julie said, startling me. She was floating in mid-air to my right, dressed in a stunning taupe dress with a sweetheart neckline. The form-fitting, satin bodice was adorned with iridescent beads and sparkling sequins; the ball gown style skirt was made of chiffon and stopped right below her knees, leaving her delicate calves exposed. Black, sequined ankle boots and what looked like a floral headdress completed the outfit. My jaw dropped. I swear I had seen the same outfit at a spring fashion show on television. How could a ghost possibly get her hands on a designer gown?

"Mouthwateringly gorgeous, isn't it?" she asked, spinning in a circle.

Mouthwateringly? Seriously, was that even a word? "Please don't tell me you went back to raid the theater," I muttered. She liked to do that a lot: sneak into the building, pick the clothes of her choice and then do that ghost thing of imagining herself in them and they'd just magically appear on her. It creeped me out big time.

"Like you'd find high fashion in the middle of nowhere." She rolled her eyes at me. "I had to go to Paris. Did you know a ghost can travel *anywhere*? Yeah, me neither."

I shook my head, not because I didn't know that tiny fact, but because I didn't understand her. "You just watched a girl die and retail therapy's your answer?"

"Don't you get all high and mighty on me," she said, crossing her arms over her chest. "I had to get the hell out of here, and you know why? Because I knew that girl." Her words surprised me. How could I have been so stupid and not see it? Julie knew everyone. I opened my mouth to speak when she cut me off. "I'm not sure how this ghost stuff works. Racing through the clouds, I realized I had to stop somewhere before I ended up in Antarctica. And that's how I stumbled to Paris. I was mad, flipping upset. Forgetting about my problems with a little distraction is my way of dealing with the pain." She raised her chin defiantly, the glint in her eyes reflecting the agony inside her. "Not only the pain of seeing a girl I knew dead, but also the pain of being trapped in limbo between life and death."

"I'm so sorry, Julie," I whispered, meaning every word. "I understand that you needed to blow off a little steam."

"It's okay." She shrugged, as though it wasn't a big deal. But it was, whether she wanted to acknowledge it, or not. "Why are you here?"

"How did you find me?" I asked, ignoring her question.

"It was pretty easy," she said, grinning. "I only had to imagine you, and there you where. I think it's similar to the disappearing thing you keep doing."

"You can teleport. Great," I muttered. So, no chance of ever hiding from her. I pointed at the shop. "You have to get me inside."

"Why? What's going on?"

"Don't know," I said, honestly. "But Maya just went in and I need to find out what she's doing."

"Okay." Julie shot me a self-assured smile and glided through the closed door. A moment later, she called in a clear and melodious voice, "I, Juliette Baron, invite you to enter this place of wisdom and mysteries. As you make your way inside, may your path be lined with wonder..." I groaned, tuning out. Gosh, she loved melodrama and attention, and would've been a Broadway star in no time.

The door opened. I entered and closed it behind me. "Thanks," I whispered.

"Should we split up?" Julie asked, hovering in mid-air, bored.

I nodded and pointed at the shop floor, signaling her to stay behind and watch the front of the shop while I checked the back. She bobbed her head so I headed for the narrow corridor that led to Elyssa's office. In front of the door, I stopped and turned the knob, then peered inside. Apart from a very tidy desk and lots of bookcases lining up the walls, the room was empty. I tried the door next to it—an overstuffed storage space—and found nothing. Where could Maya have gone? And then I remembered the staircase leading to the basement.

Scanning the empty hall one more time, I held my breath to listen for any sounds. When nothing stirred, I opened the door to the basement and tiptoed down the stairs as my hands brushed the wall to find the light switch. My fingers connected with it when something hard hit me over the head with such vigor I lost my balance and toppled down the stairs. It wasn't so much the pain but the shock at the realization that someone just hit me that kept me petrified for a moment. In that instant, as I sat up and my eyes fought to adjust to the darkness around me, a strange sensation seeped under my clothes and touched my skin, leaving a hint of gloom and doom behind.

I peered around me at nothing but pitch black. Slowly but steadily my surroundings began to take shape: the buildings below me with their closed shutters, the cobblestone streets lined with picturesque cottages, the vast abyss to my left. And then I realized where I was:

Alone on top of the wall with the strange, hurricane-like wind moving toward me at a fast speed. Letting out a tiny yelp, I crawled backwards as my mind fought to come up with a strategy to get away from here as quickly as possible. That's when the first breeze caressed my skin and sent a shiver down my spine. A strong sense of desperation washed over me. I could think of nothing but taking the plunge once and for all, ready to give up everything and everyone just to get rid of the melancholy grabbing hold of my heart.

Don't, a voice in my head screamed. But it was too late. I couldn't fight it. It was too strong.

Ever so slowly, I stepped forward to embrace the darkness descending upon me.

The End...for now.

Shadow Blood
Preview

The Swiss Alps – around witching hour

When Death comes knocking on your door you don't run or hide, you don't grab your rosary and crawl into your safest corner to pray because no one will come to your aid. I should know for I have seen the future times and times again. My name's Patricia and I'm a fallen angel. Together with a select group of supernatural beings—a coven of vampires, Lucifer's daughter, a shape shifter, a voodoo priestess, a ghost, and a necromancer—I'm destined to save humanity in its darkest hour. But before you can be saved, blood will stain the streets and no amount of rain will be able to wash it away and no thunder will be able to stifle your screams of pain upon facing the evil that is about to be unleashed upon the world.

And so the Prophecy of Morganefaire begins.

***

A few days later at Blue Moon

Silence had fallen when darkness first descended. The air reeked of filth, a pungent smell refined with the fragrance of herbs and fallen leaves. The first sensation Rebecca Duboire felt when she opened her eyes was a gnawing, all-consuming hunger that let her scream out with pain. Her hands moved up to protect herself from another agonizing wave when she knocked her elbow against something hard. Her fingers pushed against the smooth surface as she tried to place the alien sensation. And then came the shock of finding herself in a tight place destined for the dead.

A coffin.

She let out another shrill scream; her fists began to pound her prison cell as hard as she could. The wood split and earth rolled inside. After what felt like an eternity, she managed to push her hand out, followed by her exhausted body, and she realized her frail body lay buried under a thick layer of damp earth.

Someone had buried her.

She frantically dug her way out, wiggling herself free before inspecting her tomb—a cave small enough to crawl but not to stand, exposed to the destroying power of the sun but well hidden from civilization so no mortal could ever venture here and find what was left of her once glorious self. Whoever buried her, knew what he was doing. She dispelled her thoughts as to who could be responsible for her predicament and focused her attention back on her surrounding and on finding a way out.

Little stones had dug themselves into her flesh, but she paid them no attention. Her whole body felt numb, dead, and that's what she'd been only a day ago. *Dead.* Until the mirror resurrected her and pushed her back into the body that once belonged to her. Apart from the strong hunch that she was about to embark on an important mission, she had no idea who she was or what that mission was all about. She had no idea why she was wearing a simple dark-gray shirt that barely covered her hips or why the sleeves and sweetheart neckline were adorned with frills that didn't really fit this century's fashion style. In fact, she couldn't remember a single detail about her life. But that's the peril of resurrection. Your memory might be gone for a moment or forever. Rebecca had no doubt that it would return the moment she needed it.

Ignoring the slicing pain in her stomach, she pushed up on her elbows and kicked away the dry earth, leaves and branches covering her. The stones dug deeper into her skin as she forced her body into a sideway position. She could smell the forest beyond the tomb. Freedom was finally within her reach.

A wafer-thin beam of light fell through a hole in the wall on the moss covering parts of the floor. Keeping her had bowed, she struggled to her knees and let her gaze trail up and down the cave, looking for an exit. A cold draught caressed her skinny ankles. She bent down and noticed a narrow aperture on the other side of the wall.

The opening was barely bigger than an oblong hole, worn out by rain, but it was big enough for her emaciated body to pass through. She pressed herself flat against the naked ground and reached out the hole, searching for something to hold on to. Her fingers clenched around a notch and she flexed her tired muscles, breathed in and out, and then pulled herself with all her might out of the cave into the black night.

The strenuous effort exhausted her so she lay on the ground for a while, gasping for air. Late twilight had transformed a dark gray sky into a magnificent curtain dotted with a few lustrous stars. She sat up on her elbows, and looked down to inspect her half-naked body. Her skin looked old and wrinkled, and felt as dry as the parchment she used to write on, stretched over protruding bones that creaked from old age. Her once luscious, dark red locks had fallen out, leaving behind round patches of flaky skin with raised edges she could feel under her fingertips. Her ribs stood out beneath the thin material of her shirt. Her once curvy body with long, shapely legs and a thin waist, had faded away. The left shin was dangerously bent, and she tried to remember if she had broken her leg before dying, but could not recall. She didn't dwell on the thought. It was nothing a little blood couldn't solve. She might seem old and ugly now, but she knew she'd soon be young and beautiful again, despite centuries of living in Hell and not feeding from the source. Her beauty might be hidden behind a thick layer of dirt and saggy skin, but a good scrub and a few drops of blood would solve those tiny problems for her, and then Rebecca's glory would once again be both admired and feared.

Without further delay she started walking. The ground was damp as if it had been raining all day. The thick mud on the sole of her feet slowed down her pace, but she didn't worry. She had at least five hours before sunrise and she was determined to find a mortal before the first ray of light fell.

Soon she reached a paved road. The night had deepened when her sharp eyes noticed two soft beams not far away from her. She stumbled forwards, eager to find out what kind of light could break a dark night. The two dots moved nearer, getting stronger, and passed without noticing her standing just a few feet away. She stopped in astonishment and stared ahead. Prior to her resurrection she had been a ghost accustomed with this century's technology, but seeing it all live overwhelmed her nonetheless.

***

At least another hour must've passed and the moon had risen to a high crescent, illuminating the dark asphalt. Rebecca's supernatural ears picked up the sound of the approaching car long before it reached her range of vision. With only the light of the bluish moon above her she began to wave, all the while concentrating her supernatural powers on influencing the driver's mind. The headlights drew nearer, accompanied by the motor's whirring sound. Rebecca kept on waving until the lights fell on her shape...and passed by. Her eyes followed it, too disappointed to notice that the driver had slowed down, coming to a halt some distance away, then changed into back gear and pulled back to the point where she was standing. A few feet away he stopped, the headlights focused on her, and then the engine revved and he sped off, probably frightened by whatever he saw in the rearview mirror. She couldn't blame him. A stranger stopping a car in the middle of nowhere was strange. An old, withered woman dressed in a thin shirt was a whole different level of suspicious.

Cars weren't her friends. They were too fast, leaving the driver the choice to speed off and escape her grip at any second. She left the road and ventured back into the surrounding woods, following an unpaved path that seemed to go on forever. For a moment, she considered the possibility to go back, and hide in the cave, but changed her mind, and stumbled toward the trees not far ahead.

The moment she reached the forest she knew she wasn't alone. She turned her head sharply and sniffed the air to catch a whiff of the stranger watching her from the shadows, but her senses were too weak to distinguish if old or new blood coursed through his veins. Nevertheless she smiled because she had a target and this one was within her reach.

The thicket moved with a mild breeze. She looked up to the sky, wrapped her arms around her waist, and strolled towards the bushes as her thin voice broke the eerie silence of the night.

"Penny, where are you?" she shouted. "Come here, doggie!" She didn't sound like a grown woman, merely like a frightened thing afraid of the dark. She figured that ought to infuse confidence and trigger anyone's protective instincts. Feigning hesitation, she took another step forward when a huge shadow rose in front of her. She let out an exaggerated gasp and fell rearwards on her back.

She could sense his hesitation and then a hand reached for her upper arm, ready to help her back to her feet. "I'm sorry. I didn't mean to startle you," a low, male voice said. She tilted her head slightly to inspect him, but it was too dark and her burned, immortal eyes were too weak to make out more than just the curve of his nape where a steady pulse thumped beneath the skin.

"What are you doing out here in the middle of the night?" he asked. "Did you get lost?" He tugged at her arm gently, as though to reassure her of his good intentions, a moment before he let go of her again.

"I'm looking for my dog. Have you seen a small, little thing with shaggy, brown hair, big eyes?" She forced a tremor into her thin voice to make it seem choked, as though she'd been crying for a while. "My baby ran away. She must be so frightened."

"I haven't seen her. How long have you been looking?"

"I don't know," she lied.

"She's probably hiding. It's too dark to find her at night. Do you live nearby?"

"I don't know where I am," she said. A few drops of moisture fell on her and gathered on the ancient skin of her head. The air was heavy with the damp scent of oncoming rain. She considered her options. Under normal circumstances she'd just attack, but the mortal seemed strong, used to the rough life out here in the woods. He fetched a torch out of his jacket and flicked it on, directing the dim light on her face, blinding her. A small gasp escaped her throat. Cupping a hand over her eyes, she blinked in succession. He averted the beam from her so she dared a look at him, which confirmed her first impression. He was well past his prime but sturdy and tall, taller than any other man she had ever seen, with short, bristly hair crowning his graying head. Weak as she was, if she wanted to take down this bull of a man, she'd need to be sneaky about it.

"You're hurt. What happened?" He sounded worried as his glance wandered down to her twisted leg. She could only imagine what she looked like, what someone must've done to her centuries ago.

And then parts of her memory came to her, together with a name.

Aidan McAllister.

He was the one she was looking for. The one who had killed her body and trapped her inside the tomb where she lay for centuries, unable to rise...until her ghost reunited the shards of the mirror and brought her back to life by connecting her immortal soul with the remnants of her once immortal body, merging the two into one piece.

"I think I fell," she said.

"Is that all?" He didn't sound convinced. She shook her head, wide-eyed, signaling she had no idea so he continued, "There's a hut nearby where I and my family stay during our vacations. My daughter's a nurse. She can help you with your leg. First thing tomorrow we'll take you to someone who'll find out what happened to you."

"But Penny's still out here," Rebecca said halfheartedly.

"We'll find her." He smiled encouragingly as she let him take her hand to guide her away from the bushes to a small winding path. Toward his family.

End of Preview. Shadow Blood will be out soon.

Printed in Great Britain
by Amazon.co.uk, Ltd.,
Marston Gate.